Nate and the New Yorker

Nate once had the love of his life, but he's met Cameron, a New York millionaire with an eccentric cross-dressing butler.

Cameron is keen to share his world of classy restaurants, Broadway shows, and fabulous parties, and while Nate's friends see the makings of a fantasy romance, it's Nate who has to learn how to open his heart again.

But is Cameron simply second best?

Nate's Last Tango

Nate's life couldn't be better. He's living with his rich boyfriend, Cameron, in New York while being wined and dined all over the city.

But when Nate decides to visit his friends back in Sydney, Cameron suggests they break it off for a while. Cam's cross-dressing butler is not impressed, and with the help of his lesbian aunt, they drag Cameron down-under to sort out his relationship and take in the sights of Mardi Gras!

With Nate at a loss to what went wrong, he faces the dim reality that love may have run its course.

Nate and the New Yorker

Yorker

&

Nate's Last Tango

Kevin Klehr

Published by
NineStar Press
PO Box 91792
Albuquerque, New Mexico, 87199
www.ninestarpress.com

Print ISBN #978-1-947139-67-1
Cover by Natasha Snow
Edited by Jason Bradley

To my beautiful man and fellow traveler, Warren.

NATE AND THE NEW YORKER

Chapter One

"I THINK PRAGUE is for lovers," said Ben. He'd just complained about how milky the coffee was in the Czech Republic, and now this. "Yeah. Prague is the place you take your one true love."

"Then what's Paris?" I asked.

"That's easy," replied Lucy. "Paris is where you have a steamy affair."

"Then I guess Amsterdam is for singles to get up to mischief," I added.

My friends stared into space as if they were pondering the meaning of life, while their goulash was getting cold. I looked at my food. The enticing mix of hearty cuisine slopped on my plate had me slobbering like a mutt. My knife cracked the surface of my deep-fried potato rösti, and as my fork made its way to my lips, it had to stop so I could take in the odor of this salty indulgence.

"Really, Nathan!" Lucy glared at me as if she was watching some kinky sex act even she'd disapprove of. "Just eat the bloody thing. I swear sex and food stimulate the same part of your brain."

I crunched hard, making sure my grin reached both ears. She rolled her eyes and shoved a huge chunk of carrot and beef in her mouth before smirking. Strange violin music came from above. As I glanced up at the tinny speaker, the middle-aged waitress who looked as if she should cut down on sampling the food sidled up to me.

"You like?"

She pointed to the speaker. I wanted to say it sounded like someone was murdering that musical instrument, but I decided to keep my mouth shut.

"My son. He practice music. Good, eh?" The three of us nodded. "I make louder." She marched away proudly.

"Eat quickly," said Ben. "That music sounds like someone is strangling a cat."

"I never pictured a woman her age wearing lilac," stated Lucy.

"Well, we are away from the tourist spots," I said. "You have to expect local charm when we eat in this district."

"And the food is better," said Ben. He waved the chunk of meat on his fork to emphasize his point. He chewed, swallowed, and then pointed at us with his knife. "What's been your favorite city on this trip?"

"Barcelona," Lucy replied.

"Yes, I agree," I said. "Amsterdam was fun. Hey, it was a lot of fun. But Barcelona is a true party town."

"Plus you got laid there."

"Yes, I did. Another notch on my bedpost."

"That's one less than me." Ben was keeping score.

"One less? You've had two encounters?"

"Well, if we'd stop going to gay clubs, maybe I could be part of this conversation," Lucy said, shaking her head while stirring her gravy.

"I know we both got laid in Amsterdam, Ben, but where else did you get laid?" I asked.

"I got laid twice in Amsterdam," he replied. "You see, there was one night I couldn't sleep and..."

"Do you guys ever give it a rest?" Lucy asked.

"Do we really need to answer that?" I replied. "So, Ben, where did you find him?"

He panted like a puppy. "All I'll say is, a leather club opened my eyes."

"You went to the leather club without me?"

"Yeah," said Lucy. "You went to the leather club without us?"

"Well, when a boy wants to play hard, you know, friends are better left behind. Besides, you two were asleep."

"How do you know? Did you check on us?"

"Of course not. What if you were awake?"

I raised my wine glass. "To my favorite slutty workmate and friend." My buddies also raised their glasses. "And to you too, Lucy, who gets plenty of sex back home in Sydney."

She grinned wickedly.

"You could have got laid in Berlin," said Ben.

"True," I added. "There was an experience I'm sure you'd never get offered back home."

"No way! That pierced guy was freaky."

"But he wanted you."

"Yeah, but for what?

"He had more holes than a target at a shooting range," Ben added.

Even lilac lady laughed. We downed our drinks before she brought another bottle.

"Just think," said Lucy. "Tomorrow we're traveling home."

"Don't talk about it," I replied. "I don't want this holiday to end."

"I'm glad we're finishing our trip in a cheap country," Ben added. "My credit card is maxed out."

"Me too."

"Me three," said Lucy.

"I don't know why you're complaining. You own the café we work in, boss. You make all the money. I'm dreading seeing my bank statement."

"Now, now, Nathan. I promised I'd get Ben to teach you how to make coffee. I need another barista. It pays better than being a waiter."

I half smiled.

"And I know you're just as fussy about coffee as I am," Ben declared. "You'll have those office workers lining up for their morning hit of caffeine. You'll be a great pusher."

"Pusher?" I asked.

"Yeah. Their addiction and your will to supply an aromatic brew of premium roasted liquid dependence will make you a top-class dealer."

"He's right," said Lucy. "Morning coffee is what keeps my café afloat."

"I just have to get used to being a morning person," I admitted. "But still, it's a sacrifice I'm prepared to make for better pay." I refilled our glasses and raised mine. "A toast to a wonderful couple of friends and a wonderful three weeks away from work!"

"Yay, Europe," said Ben. "Well, at least the little we've seen of it." He clinked my glass.

"I'll drink to that." Lucy swirled her wine before she drank. "And you guys have been great travel companions."

"Thank you, boss."

"And will you two stop calling me boss? I'd like to think I'm more to you than that."

"You are, boss."

She stared at Ben with murderous eyes. "Do you enjoy working at the café?"

"You can't fire me. I have to teach Nathan how to make coffee."

"You're right. I'll wait until after you teach him." She poked her tongue out.

"So, shall we do the same thing next year?" I asked. "Maybe South America? Or shall we keep the cost down and discover Asia?" I sipped. "What about...?"

"Did you run out of battery power?" Lucy asked.

"What are you looking at?" Ben queried. He turned to see what made me pause midsentence.

The culprit stood at the entrance of the restaurant. Shortly cropped dark hair. Rosy lips curved as if a sculptor had created them by smoothing their surface with the tip of his finger. His stylishly knitted red sweater hung loosely, making his upper body a mystery. And his thick black-rimmed glasses had me picturing him on my couch, reading quietly before I'd slowly pull them off his face, exposing my own superhero.

"Nathan, are you home?" Lucy asked.

The man saw me, smiled, and then made his way to the closest empty table.

"Are you dining alone?" Ben called out to him.

I gulped my wine, nearly spilling some on my food. Then I choked. My dream man rushed over. Lucy pounded me hard on my upper back. I felt like a slab of steak getting tenderized. He gave me a glass of water. I took it, drinking steadily.

"Are you okay?" he said in an American accent.

"Yes," I whispered through strained vocal cords. "Thanks for the water."

"My pleasure." He gazed at me, mystic eyes behind dark frames.

"His name is Nathan," said my boss. "And I'm Lucy. And this is Ben."

"I'm Cameron." We all shook hands before he pulled up a chair. "What's with this violin music?"

"See that lilac-clad waitress?" Ben replied. "It's her son's music she's boring us with."

We all stared in her direction. She waved cheerfully before fishing around for an extra glass. She brought it over. Ben poured the wine.

"So why are you dining alone?" I finally found the courage to speak.

"Time away to clear my head."

"From what?"

"My family. Sometimes I just need a break from them."

"So, you came to Prague?"

"It's a bit of a distance, I know, but I wanted a place I could daydream in. And a friend suggested Prague."

"Good choice," said Lucy.

"Are you going anywhere else after Prague?" I asked.

"I don't know. I've had some suggestions from the backpackers at my hostel, but I'm open to ideas."

"Well, we're just ending our short trip. We've been to Barcelona, Berlin, Paris, Amsterdam, and now here."

"Have you got plans for tonight, Cameron?" Lucy asked.

"Not at the moment, no." His eyes wandered in my direction as he spoke.

Ben raised his hand to get lilac lady's attention. "Bill, please."

"Don't you mean check?"

"You say tom-ay-to, we say tom-ah-to," replied Ben.

"You say bell pepper, we say capsicum," Lucy added.

"You say duvet, we say doona," I said. "And the list goes on and on."

"I see," he replied. "We say check, you say bill. Got it. But do you need to go so soon?"

Lucy pointed at me. "Oh, he's staying here. Ben and I need to go and..." She searched thin air for the end of her sentence.

"We need to go and find somewhere to do our laundry," Ben continued. "It's been a long trip."

"At this hour?"

"Hey, there's a river up the road. We can wash our underwear in the water."

"But you haven't finished your dinner."

"We're full," said Lucy unconvincingly.

My friends stood, made their way to the waitress, and paid for our meals. As they left, Lucy blew me a kiss.

"I recommend the goulash, Cameron. It's really good."

"Can I taste yours?"

I fed his curvy lips. He chewed slowly, never taking his eyes off me. "What do you think?"

"I think you're almost done, Nathan, and you'd be watching me eat if I ordered now."

Lilac woman brought over a small plate of the local stew, then picked up the wine bottle and refilled our glasses. We thanked her as she smiled kindly.

"You've got no choice now," I said.

We clinked glasses.

"I guess that makes it official," he said.

"You guess this makes what official?"

"I'm on a date with a charismatic guy called Nathan."

Chapter Two

"WHY IS THAT one offering her a book?" Cameron asked.

We stood on the Charles Bridge analyzing one particular statue. Madonna cradled her child while reaching out to a curly haired man in robes who seemed to be ready to help her off her pedestal. Another man was attempting to show her an open text, which she paid no attention to.

"I think the book has a true definition of a virgin," I replied. "And he's questioning her virtue."

"You're wicked, Nathan."

"Hey, there must have been people that questioned her story."

"Well, what about that one?" He pointed to a male figure with a metal ring around its head. Gold stars decorated the statue's headdress as he carried an ornamental Jesus nailed to a cross.

"He's a collector of religious artifacts," I replied. "And he's got enough saviors in his home to keep the zombie apocalypse from his door."

Cameron kissed me on the cheek, startling me. A woman in a long fawn coat stopped briefly with open jaw. She turned from us and kept walking.

"I keep forgetting that the Eastern Bloc is overly religious," said my charming American.

"Well, they have to learn to be open-minded sometime."

I reached for his cheeks and lured his curved lips to mine. He enchanted me as I hid in a world just big enough for two. Cool air traced the maze-like contours of my ears, sending my body into a brief shiver. He cradled my cheeks with lukewarm hands while heating my ears with the warmth of his mittens.

We parted lips. Behind him, the sky was sprinkled with stars as if the gods had haphazardly shaken salt into the blue as part of a magic ritual. More statues peered in our direction, approving of our mutual attraction. And diamonds sparkled on the surface of the river, ready for the more earnest figurines to hide under their robes when no one was looking.

"This is a beautiful city," he said.

"It's made for lovers, Cameron."

"Even if this is only a short meeting."

"Hush. Let's walk." I took his hand boldly, then lost myself in his coffee-toned eyes. Designer frames could not hide their soulful glint. We stepped forward as he gazed into my secrets for one night.

"What do you think of this one?" I asked. Three pained-looking statues with their wrists bound in metal and ropes looked to the heavens.

"They're in limbo for not ever knowing love."

"That's kind of deep and poetic. I didn't expect that from you."

"Oh, I can be shallow when I want to be, Nathan. I read gossip columns magazines while listening to NPR in my spare time."

"So, you're shallow while you read and intellectual while you listen?"

"Back home I mix highbrow and lowbrow constantly. Both have their place, although my parents wouldn't agree."

"What are they like?"

"They're the original fun police. Any hairbrained notion from me and they're on my case. You should have seen their faces when I said I was visiting Prague. My father eyed me sternly, mouthing off about potential business opportunities in London and Zurich."

"Business opportunities? What is it you do, Cameron?"

"At the moment, I'm a hopeless drifter enjoying a night with a dreamy Australian in Prague."

I could feel my face go red against the frosty air. He kissed my cheek again, leaving a moist lip-shaped outline. We continued to stroll.

"Cameron, where in the US do you live?"

"New York."

"Manhattan?"

"Yes."

"Who do you live with?"

"I'm alone."

"Are you in a rent-controlled apartment?"

"I'm comfortable enough."

More statues watched us from the balcony of St Salvator Church. We wandered past an archway and entered.

Electric lights painted the place of worship in tones of yellow. The arched windows stood like tall anorexic giants, allowing the stars to direct their glow through their eyes of glass. Intricately carved pews faced the altar like rows in a theatre, awaiting weary travelers eager to be treated with a spectacle. The woman who regarded us after we had kissed on the bridge sat on one of the honey-toned benches, mumbling as she prayed.

"And here we face the one who will judge us," said Cameron.

"I never knew God wore an evening coat."

"Fashion should be important when you're a deity. It presents a good example to your followers."

I smirked. "I literally don't have a comeback for that. You've stumped me."

"That would be the first time I've done that tonight, Nathan." He took a quick peek at our nemesis. "Should we kiss again?"

"Why not? She's the only other person here."

So we did, and her gibberish spoken behind cupped palms became louder. But I drowned out the noise as I sunk deeper into his core. He enticed my naughty alter ego with his masculine breath and hands that clutched my sides like a trap. He was ready for worship. With one masterful stroke, I could unzip his manhood and give it breathing space.

"I have to stop, Nathan," he said. "I'm having really dirty thoughts."

"Um, me too."

Our jury of one let out an audible breath. We stared at her like vultures waiting for their prey to die. She pointed to an image of her savior on the ceiling.

"I'm sure he approves," I said. So I blew the son of God a kiss. She prayed louder.

We left the cathedral but not before kissing once more, and we felt the cobbled streets under our feet as we slowly made our way to Cameron's hostel. Horses clopped along, taking tourists on their way through this magical town. The Pickpocket Express, a name given to one of the local trams by travel guides, snaked its way past us. The storybook buildings had me searching for Puss in Boots, Cinderella, and various Prince Charmings.

"This is a city frozen in time," I said. "A place that could be under a glass dome, paused in the course of history."

"Why is it so beautiful, Nathan?"

"It was never bombed during the Second World War. Apparently Hitler considered it too pretty."

"Oh no."

"Oh yes, and it was lucky for Prague that he thought so."

"That's not what I meant when I said 'oh no'."

He looked as if he had seen a ghost. Instead, he was watching a white limousine cruise slowly toward us. As the driver side window lowered, a middle-aged red-haired gent with a nose you could ski off addressed him.

"I've been looking for you all night, sir."

"I needed some breathing space, Roger."

"I appreciate that you needed some time out, sir, but you could have told me. You know how your parents react every time they find out you're not with me."

"But they're back in New York, Roger. Chill out."

I waved to the driver.

"Oh, sorry. Nathan, this is Roger."

"His butler."

"My butler."

My charming American looked at me as if I had discovered he had no penis. "You're wealthy, I take it?" I asked.

"More than I'd like to admit."

"It is late, sir, and we have a schedule tomorrow."

"I'm so sorry about this, Nathan." His face now resembled a baseball player who didn't make it to first base. "This is not the way I wanted the night to end."

"Nor me."

We kissed with a connection stronger than Lego. And that scared me. Fortunately, Roger marred the moment by clearing his throat. "Sorry to trouble the both of you," he said, "but there is a big day planned tomorrow."

Cameron stepped back. "This conversation isn't over yet, is it?"

"No," I replied.

"Roger, hand me a card." He passed it to me, and in Art Deco text it simply read: Cameron Charlton, followed by various phone numbers and an email address.

"I was hoping to spend the night with you," I said. I felt as sad as a puppy being ignored.

"Call me."

"But you live in New York, and I live in Sydney."

"Nathan, I've had a taste. That's not where I intend to leave things. In fact, what's your number?"

I told him, then after one last peck on the lips, he slipped away with his butler. As for me, I watched the car trail away into the fairy-tale town.

Chapter Three

"WE SHOULD HAVE ended our trip in Singapore," Ben said. "It's closer to our own time zone."

"You know we debated this," Lucy replied. "Although now that we're facing the long journey home with stopovers in Frankfurt and Singapore, we really should have planned better."

They both stared at me as if lasers would shoot from their eyes, using me as their target.

"Okay, I'm sorry," I said. "I just wanted to spend as much time in Europe as possible."

We sat in economy as an airline stewardess who was obviously employed for her efficiency and not her looks marched down the aisle to check our seat belts.

"I feel like we're on a military plane," said Lucy. "Did you see the way she looked me up and down as I showed her my ticket?"

"It's the hat, darling," Ben replied. "Your complicated traveling hat."

"I think it's chic."

"It would be chic if it was a lot smaller," I said. "It grows out of your head like an oversized mushroom."

"Well, I couldn't fit it in my luggage."

"Too much shopping," said Ben.

She sighed, took off the black lace bonnet, and placed it in her lap.

"I take?" queried the stewardess.

"Um."

"Go on, Lucy," I said. "It's not a security blanket."

My friend reluctantly handed her precious headpiece to the staff member and watched in horror as she slammed it into an overhead compartment without checking to see if it would fit.

"There was luggage in there!" she squealed. "My hat will be out of shape."

"I'm sure she knows what she's doing," said Ben. "Now calm down. It's only until we get to Frankfurt. Then you can place it under your seat on our international flights."

"But it's the height of Berlin fashion."

"I swear, you stress out more than a gay guy."

Ben flicked through the in-flight magazine, checking out the models in the advertisements. Without looking up to me, he nonchalantly alleged, "So, Nathan. You now have two notches on your travel bedpost."

Lucy peered at me.

"Nope. It didn't happen."

Ben slowly turned his head, and Lucy repeated my words as if it was she who missed out. "It didn't happen. How could it not happen?"

"He's a time waster," said Ben.

"His butler showed up."

"His butler showed up?" Lucy queried. "I'm sure I heard him say he was staying at a hostel."

"He was covering up. Apparently he's rich."

"Did he give you his contact details?" asked Ben.

"Hey, you just said he was a time waster."

"That's before the words 'Sugar Daddy' came to mind."

"What does he do?" Lucy asked.

"I have no idea. I think he avoided the question."

"Mafia?" Ben said.

"No, he's too young," Lucy replied.

"How old do you have to be to join the Mafia?"

"Perhaps he's a drug dealer. Did you think of that, Nathan?"

"Guys, you're blowing this thing out of proportion," I said. "Why would a drug dealer be in Prague? This is hardly a city with a cocaine problem."

"An antiques dealer?" Ben suggested.

"Now that I could live with. But we're on our way home, so my date didn't turn into a romance."

"Can you look him up?" Lucy asked. "What's his surname? We can google him."

"I have his contact details."

"Then what are you waiting for?"

"Look, he was cute. We walked around the city. It was romantic. But it'll be filed in my memory as my night with an American dreamer. Let's forget about it."

I ripped the card in two and raised my hand to get the stewardess's attention. Ben tried to snatch the torn pieces from me, but I extended my arm into the aisle, nearly hitting an inattentive passenger in the crotch.

The stewardess looked me up and down like a disapproving headmistress before striding over. She told the other passenger to go back to his seat, while grabbing the card from my hand and nearly breaking my fingers at the same time.

"You may have spent the night with an American dreamer," said Lucy, "but the problem is, you're not a dreamer yourself."

"I'm just taking the night for what it was. A short date that didn't follow through."

"Now, Nathan, get real!" Ben sounded more like a parent than a friend. "Lucy's right. I'm teaching you how to make coffee when we get back. What a stunning career that will be. Early mornings and grumpy office workers. You'll be steaming milk and beating yourself up over the one that got away."

"Just because he's rich is no reason to chase him."

"Yes, it is!" Both friends spoke in unison.

"Look at it this way," said Lucy. "Even if he's not Mister Right, he may introduce you to Mister Right who also happens to have a healthy bank balance."

"But you'll never know because you just threw his contact details away."

I gazed down the aisle. I considered asking the stewardess for the ripped card, but I was scared she'd drag me out of my seat and stick my nose in the garbage bin, laughing as she made me dig for the pieces.

My pocket vibrated with a funky soul tune. I pulled out my phone. I didn't recognize the number, but I answered the call without thinking twice.

"Nathan, is that you?" It was Cameron.

"Yes, it is."

"Sorry I didn't call you back last night. My cell ran out of juice. I just noticed your call. Where are you?"

"On a plane heading for Frankfurt."

"Is that your next destination? I thought Prague was your last stop in Europe."

"Your phone should be switched off," the stewardess shouted.

I covered the mouthpiece. "Sorry, I thought it was switched off."

"What did you say?" asked Cameron.

"I can't talk long. I have to switch off my phone."

"I'm sorry about last night. I really did want to take you back to my hotel."

"So what happened to the hostel you were telling us about over dinner?"

"Please, sir, your phone!" She crossed her arms.

"Look, Nathan, there's a lot I have to explain to you. When's your next trip to the Northern Hemisphere?"

"I don't know. It's not something I can just do on a whim."

"Oh, I see. Will you call me when you get home? I had a great time last night."

The flight attendant was making her way toward me like a stormtrooper. I unhitched my seat belt and briskly made my way to the back of the plane.

"I had a great time too, Cameron, and yes, of course I'll ring you when I get back to Sydney."

"Sir, your phone!"

"I'll be thirty seconds, I promise."

She tapped her foot.

"Who is that, Nathan?"

"My very own dominatrix in an airline uniform."

"Are you naked?"

"Cameron!"

She towered above me like the schoolyard bully.

"Look, I've got to go. I'm being told to hang up in no uncertain terms."

"Okay, sweetheart. Just don't forget to ring me as soon as you get home."

"Okay, darling, I will."

"I'm a lucky guy. You know that, don't you, Nathan?"

"I think I'm the lucky one."

"Oh, I don't know. I must have done something right to have met you."

"You are a charmer."

The stewardess snatched my phone. "Now Miss Charming, this man has to sit down with his seat belt on!" She suddenly raised her eyebrows, probably surprised to hear a man's voice on the other end of my phone.

"Yes, yes, you want to see him again. Yes, yes, he a nice-looking man, I guess. Yes, he will ring you when he goes back to Australia."

I reached for my phone, but she headed up the aisle, never looking back, and only returned it to me when we landed in Frankfurt.

Chapter Four

A HEAP OF laundry as large as a volcano greeted me next to the washing machine. I eyed it like an ageing cheetah, too weary to attack. I picked at a shirt, examining the stain on the sleeve.

"I should have paid to get these washed in Prague."

I pulled at the sleeve, gradually working the shirt out of the pile. It slipped to the floor. I left it and decided I'd arrange a stack of whites to soak in bleach. I dived in, tugging at more clothes to separate into wash loads. Soon I had my gentle cycle pile, my normal wash pile, and the stuff I wasn't too sure about.

I set the machine and threw in the first load. "That should do it."

"Did you say something, Nathan?" Elliot screeched from somewhere in the apartment.

"I was talking to myself."

"You're doing that a lot lately."

"I thought I was alone." I grabbed a bucket from the cupboard under the sink, added water and bleach, and crammed my whites into it. As I closed the laundry door behind me, I noticed Elliot on my lounge. "What are you doing here?"

"Checking up on you, my darling."

"Your darling? Elliot, we haven't been an item for years."

"Yes, but I miss you when I'm not here. You were the best friend I ever had."

"Times move on. Learn to let go."

He pouted before running his fingers through his hair, making an adorable blond curl bounce on his forehead. I grinned, remembering why I had once been in love with him.

"So how was your trip?" he asked.

"Fantastic. Amsterdam is a bit of a haze, but I think I fell in love in Prague."

"You fell in love?"

"Yes, with Prague."

"That's not what you said, Nathan."

"Yes, it is." Had *I said that?*

"No, it's not. You said you fell in love *in* Prague."

"Prague was a romantic city, but I didn't fall in love."

"Did you get laid?"

"Elliot! That wasn't the purpose of our trip."

"Ah, so you did get laid."

"Elliot!"

"Who was he?"

I sighed. "Someone so butch he uses the leftover bones from his steaks as toothpicks."

"That's not your type, Nathan."

"I know, but Amsterdam does some strange things to people. It makes you stretch your boundaries."

"You had no trouble stretching mine."

"Elliot!"

"Still, I know you better than anyone, Nathan. We were together for several years."

"And they were very happy years."

I often thought of Elliot as a himbo, but he was *my* himbo, although I never used those words directly to him. He would say things from time to time that made no sense, but they kept me intrigued as I tried to work out his meaning. At the same time, I smiled fondly at his wayward musings. But somehow his beguiling logic had waned during recent visits.

The MGM lion roared from my phone. It was a text message.

Nathan, what's your e-mail address? Love, your charming American.

I typed my contact details.

Thanks. Check your inbox in ten minutes. Cam.

"Who was that?" asked Elliot.

"Just a friend."

"Nathan, I know your looks. I know your 'I'm hungry' look. I know your 'I'm horny' look. They're pretty similar. I know your 'I'm stressed' look. I answered your 'horny' and 'stressed' looks the same way. But that look, Nathan, that look is the look you used to give me when I said something you didn't understand."

I met his gaze, feeling like I somehow cheated by reading my text messages. He looked to the floor, turning the corners of his mouth down. "You have a lover, Nathan."

"I don't. Seriously, I don't."

"So who's the message from?"

"A guy I met." I oddly choked on the last word.

Elliot forced a smile. "I am your ex, after all. It's not up to me who you should see or who you shouldn't see."

I sat next to him. "You know I love you dearly," I said. "You were the person who taught me how to love. Before you, I wasn't sure how to factor someone into my life, but you showed me how easy it was."

"And *you* showed me how to come out of my shell, Nathan. You taught me to just say what was on my mind without thinking twice, and you'd listen. You helped me find my voice."

"We were a good team, weren't we?"

He started playing with the curl on his forehead. "Yes, we *were* a good team."

My funky ringtone sounded. It was Cameron, so I excused myself and took the call in my bedroom.

"Have you opened your email?" was the first thing he blurted out.

"No, I've been doing my laundry so I haven't had time to look."

"Well, are you going to check?"

"Hold on."

I tapped on the email icon and saw Cameron's message at the top of the list. I opened it, reading the first line several times in disbelief. "You charming American, what were you thinking?"

"Surprised?"

"Speechless, more like it."

"So, humor me."

"I'll consider it, Cam. I'll let you know."

"Okay, but don't keep me in the dark too long, Nathan."

"I won't. I promise."

"Bye for now, gorgeous."

"Bye for now."

I stood in my bedroom. I was in the eye of a tornado named confusion, and no matter which direction I went, I'd be sucked into No Man's Land. Should I ask Elliot for his opinion? I slowly made my way back to my guest, but he wasn't on the couch.

"Elliot!" I called. No answer. I checked the kitchen. He wasn't there either.

It seemed he'd decided to leave quietly. Strange, as most of the time it was impossible to get rid of him.

Chapter Five

DROPPING A BOMBSHELL is an art. Some simply blurt it out and watch the carnage. Others time it so it slips in discreetly, and they wait for the delayed reactions around the room, like observing a row of dominoes fall one by one. And then there's me.

Ben and I met at Lucy's a little while after Elliot visited. The following day we'd all be back at work in her café, but that night we were having cheap pasta and cask wine as we relived our trip.

"Remember those bears all over Berlin?" Ben asked. He swirled his bolognaise on his fork with robotic accuracy and shoved it in his mouth.

"Yes, they were gorgeous!" replied our host. "I wanted to take one home with me. It would have looked good in my bathroom."

"In your bathroom?" I queried.

"I'm not sure I could cope with a brightly colored bear sculpture staring at me as I'm sitting on your toilet," said Ben.

"You could ask it to fetch toilet paper when you run out," Lucy replied.

"Imagine going through customs with it." I sprinkled parmesan over my dish between thoughts. "Would it be luggage, or would we have to pay an extra fare and seat it next to us? Still, one would look pretty cool in your bathroom, and hey, the way you collect things, it wouldn't be the weirdest thing in your apartment."

The sharp tang of cheese awoke me as the creamy sauce spread like lava on my tongue. Strands of spaghetti swam through the tangy tomato, before a hint of basil added the zest that took me to culinary nirvana.

"Oh for goodness sake, Nathan!" cried Lucy. "It's sauce from a jar and dried spaghetti. Stop having an orgasm over your food."

"But you put fresh basil on top. Not the dried stuff."

"Yeah, I had to make prepackaged bolognaise sauce edible while keeping within my budget."

I scrutinized the fork I was using. Its milky-colored handle was a replica of antique bone cutlery, while the brown clay bowl I was eating out of could have been a throwback to the 1970s. It was probably made by some hippies who had forged their own paradise in a forest somewhere.

"Nathan, what's on your mind?" Ben asked.

"Why do you think something's on my mind?"

"Because when you're enjoying your food, you look like you're making love to it. But when something's on your mind, you stop eating and examine the closest thing you can find."

I thrust spaghetti into my mouth.

"You're not getting off the hook that easily," Lucy said. "What's on your mind?"

I swallowed, then gulped down half a glass of wine.

"Cameron sent me business-class tickets to visit him in New York."

Ben nearly coughed up his food. "He did *what*?"

"You have to go," declared Lucy. I scrunched my lips. "Nathan, I can find another waiter while you're gone. When are you going?"

"Monday night. For a week."

"You leave in five days!"

"You can take two suitcases on business class, you know," added Ben.

"I'm not sure if I'm going." I could have confessed to being a serial killer by the way my friends glared at me. "Look, it was a whirlwind romance. Hey, it wasn't even that. It was a couple of hours with a charming American."

"A charming American who's bought you return flights to visit him." Lucy was shaking her head as she said this. "What's there to consider?"

"It sounds like the plot of a cheap romance novel."

"Yes, Nathan, but it's your cheap romance novel. Most of us would sell our souls to star in our own romance. You didn't even get to first base, and he still wants to take it further."

"I don't really remember what he looks like."

"Brown eyes. Brown hair. Nice package," said Ben. "Now, what's your next issue?"

"I don't know if I like him."

"You liked him the night you met."

"But I was adding an exclamation mark at the end of our European trip. Now he's after more. What if I'm not ready?"

My friends shared glances. Then Ben pointed to Lucy as a gesture for her to speak next. She put her bowl on the coffee table.

"Nathan. Darling, lovable, confused Nathan. Some of us read storybooks when we were young. Common girls born on the wrong side of the track would somehow cross paths with a prince, and they'd fall in love and live happily ever after." She looked at Ben, and he gave her an approving nod. "And you know what, Nathan? Those stories resonate with us the rest of our lives."

"But..."

"Don't interrupt, Nathan. You were about to say that finding a prince is mere fantasy. Finding real-world goals and achieving them for ourselves is how to keep control of one's life. That way there's no second player you have to rely on."

"Yeah, but..."

"But, Nathan, you have been independent for long enough. And where has it gotten you? You're a waiter in my café. And why are you a waiter in my café? Because all your efforts to find a real job have resulted in short-term contracts. Am I making myself clear, Nathan?"

"I know what you're saying, Lucy, but..."

"Oh, for goodness sake! Nathan, if you step foot through the door of my café on Monday, you're fired!"

I looked to Ben. He nodded with a gleeful grin. Then I clutched my wine glass, wondering what Elliot would have to say.

Chapter Six

"I REMEMBER THIS song," said Elliot. "This was one of our songs."

The playlist echoed from my sound system. I stopped making my morning coffee to listen to the track. He was right. We had tried to waltz to it on a footpath outside a shop that was playing it. Ever since, that melancholy tune reminded me of a time when Elliot's hair was just a little too long and that curl hid his left eye. I had kept brushing it aside as we'd continued to dance.

I poured milk in my coffee and then joined him on the sofa. "You're here early," I said. "It's hardly brunch time."

"I saw you were home and thought I'd say hello. You're not sick or anything, are you? I mean, shouldn't you be at work?"

"I'm taking the day off."

Elliot kicked his shoes off and crossed his legs on my couch. He stared past me with sad eyes. I sat quietly too, noting the aroma of my fresh brew. An up-tempo number began as he closed his eyes and gently swayed.

"Nathan, remember this one? I didn't like it at first, but you convinced me to listen. I thought the vocals were singing a melody the beat hadn't found. But you made me listen to it. Really listen to it. You told me to think of the voice as the orchestration and the beat as a lost child finding his way home. You were always open when it came to music. And you were right. It's a mother's voice calling to her child."

"What was I on when I said that?"

He looked right through me. "Life. You were high on life."

I lost the taste for my coffee as it was getting cold. I smiled at Elliot. He was wearing a ridiculous striped top, with the lines running horizontally. He looked like *Where's Waldo?* and just needed a beanie to complete the picture. But this was his unique style. I had battled with it initially, picking out other things for him to wear. I'd finally warmed to his taste.

"Don't think I didn't notice the suitcase on your bed, Nathan."

"I'm taking a short trip."

"Melbourne? Perth?"

"New York."

"That's not a short trip. That's a fifteen-hour flight."

"It's longer. Six hours longer. There's a stopover."

"The jetlag will kill you. How long are you away?"

"Only one week."

Elliot stretched out, placing his feet on the floor. "What's this classical music playing?"

"Oh, it's something I heard in Prague. Our waitress's son had recorded it on a violin, and it was bad. But then I hummed what I thought it sounded like to an old man who regularly comes into the café. He catalogs music at a classical station. He knew it right away. He left it on a memory stick for me and told Lucy to make sure I got it."

"You had a strange smirk when you told that story, Nathan."

"Did I? Well, it's a strange story." I felt uneasy, so I stood and made my way to the microwave to reheat my coffee.

"Why don't we have sex?" Elliot asked. His voice was as casual as if suggesting a trip to the movies.

"What? Why? You're my ex."

I stepped out from the kitchen and peered at him. He studied me sadly once again. The bell on the microwave sounded so I took out my cup and decided to take solace by sitting up on the laminate bench.

"Some gay men continue sex after the romance is gone. It's healthy."

"How can it be healthy?"

"Because old lovers make perfect friends."

"That's not a reason to have sex."

"What I mean is, it's healthier to have sex with someone you know well."

"We are not having sex. Elliot, you have to let go. I'm your ex."

Silence. A torch song about old lovers played on my stereo. The silky female vocals sang of a connection that was hard to break. I shuddered, feeling alone in my kitchen.

"Nathan, who is he?"

"Who is who?"

The MGM lion roared.

"The man from Prague. The one you've packed a suitcase for. The one who just texted you."

I read the message.

Your plane leaves in three hours. Safe travels.
Love, that charming American.

I took one very deep breath.

"Remind me why we broke up, Nathan."

"Because you like the original film version of *Hairspray*, and I liked the musical."

"Opposites attract."

"But rarely ever stay together."

"I don't know why we can't have sex!" He shouted this. His pained voice both touched and irked me.

"Elliot, we are not together anymore!" I screamed. A tear wet my cheek. "Now get out of my apartment. I have a plane to catch."

Chapter Seven

"WHY ARE YOU still awake?" I asked. Cameron had the energy of a toddler. "It's way past your bedtime."

"Roger helped me readjust my body clock over the last five days."

"He did what?"

"My evening is your morning, so Roger has taught me to sleep when you're asleep and wake when you get up."

"Cameron, you're sweet, but you have way too much time on your hands."

This was my first night in his high-rise Manhattan apartment. It looked like a warehouse conversion, although I knew it was impossible for a warehouse to be this many stories high. Dark metallic window frames outlined views of elegant Art Deco architecture. The charcoal buildings made me believe I was in a noir film, as shonky cops and eccentric villains hid in the shadows below. Or at least in my jetlagged state, that's what I imagined.

"I'm surprised you don't own a penthouse," I said.

"Nathan, if I could afford a penthouse, I would have sent a private plane to pick you up from Sydney."

"Still, I thought…"

"You thought that it would be bigger. Three bedrooms are enough for me. One for me, one for guests, and one for Roger."

I sat on his black modular lounge and stared at the moon. Its crescent shape hung, suspended against a navy cardboard sky. Its tip pointed into the window of the nearest towering skyscraper. Inside, a woman snuggled next to an older man, cheek to cheek with her arm around his chest, lit by the multicolored hues of a television screen.

"That could be us one day," said the charming American. "They're always parked on the couch doing something. Reading. Watching TV. Talking."

"We've just met, Cameron. We're not quite lovers yet."

"Then I have until the end of the week to change your mind."

"That's what I like about you. You're a dreamer."

He stood and reached for my hand, peering like a bride through the veil of the reflected stars painted on his glasses. What an odd thought. Gosh, I was jetlagged! His dreamy lips, the color of strawberry milk, puckered as I rose from my comfort zone on the couch. We kissed. His lips charged me like caffeine, taking some of the sleep from my body. Our lips parted.

"Roger!" he called.

"Yes, sir?"

"We're going for a walk."

"We are?"

"Yes, we are, Nathan. If you go to bed now, you'll wake in the middle of the night when your body thinks it should be awake. So we're staying up for a while." He fluttered his eyelids at Roger. "Be a dear and make that special dessert before you go to bed. I want to share it with my elegant Australian."

"Elegant?"

"What about stylish Australian?"

"Hah. Let's work on that adjective, Cam."

He nodded. "Roger, make sure you get a good sleep. After days of changing my sleep patterns, yours should get back to normal."

"That's fine, sir. I have just the sedative to help me."

"Good to hear. Now, Nathan, let's go for that walk."

NEON SIGNS SPRUIKING a 24-hour delicatessen, Little Poland, and various ATMs floated past in a landscape that looked like Sesame Street at night. Pastries tempted pedestrians into a store where bakers had settled in for a long shift. Rich caramel and jam oozed out of triangular-shaped delights. White icing hugged twisted miniature cakes, enticing a homeless man to tap on the window.

Bagels spread out in another shop window, with a sign claiming they were the best in Manhattan. A busker rapped between the notes he played on his saxophone, telling us God would love us if we bought his CDs. And all this was happening as cars breezed along on the wrong side of the street.

"What's the matter, Nathan?"

I pointed to the pavement. "It's not raining, yet there's drops on the footpath."

"That's chewing gum from decades ago."

"Really!"

"Really."

I tried to kick one of the dark spots off, but it had made its home and was never leaving. "So where are we going, Cameron?"

"Right here." He opened a glass door and let me enter first.

"Mr. Charlton," said an eager young woman who darted straight to us. "I have your table ready."

We were inside a smart French restaurant, with staff emerging like the military in crisp black uniforms and leading us to our table, covered with an intricate lace cloth.

Our waitress lit the two tall white candles. "May I offer a drink to begin with?" she asked. "Our cocktail selection is second to none."

"Nathan?" My charming American wanted me to choose.

"What do you recommend?" I asked her.

She rubbed her chin. "You look like a Watermelon Tingle type of guy."

"Has it got vodka in it?"

"Yes."

"Make that two," Cameron replied.

She slipped away and left us to study the menu.

"Yikes, look at these prices!"

"What's the matter with them? Too shabby? We can go somewhere nicer, but I was going to take you upmarket tomorrow night."

"No, Cameron. These prices are just fine. Expensive, but fine. I guess this is just petty cash to you."

He pouted like a sad circus clown. "Nathan, while you're with me for the next week, I don't want to hear any talk about money."

I felt like a balloon someone had popped. "Cam, while I'm with you in New York, I want to pay my own way."

"Can you afford your meal?"

"Not here. Can we go somewhere else?"

"This is one of my favorite restaurants. I'm showing you *my* city. Can you at least chill? Either that or order a lettuce leaf."

"Okay, I'm sorry. I'm being ungrateful. Thank you for bringing me here."

He half grinned. "Good. Do you know what you want for starters and entrée?"

"Cameron, a starter and an entrée are the same thing. You mean, do I know what I want for entrée and mains?"

He gazed at me as if I'd landed from another planet. "Nathan, an entrée is a main meal."

"But isn't entrée French for entry? Like the entry to your meal?"

"I'm not sure." He looked above as if the answer was floating near his head. "I guess you say entrée, and I say starters."

"I guess. How will this relationship ever work?"

"Nathan, you do everything back to front down under."

"That sounds like a sexual position."

He smirked. A drink redder than a watermelon fizzed in front of me. We clinked glasses before I took a sip. The lush juice painted the roof of my mouth like a fountain. As it trickled down my throat, it rejuvenated my spirit, making my eyes widen like a voyeur's at a peep show.

"Wow, you really like that cocktail."

"I have an unholy love affair with food, or so Lucy keeps telling me."

"Do you know what you want for dinner?" asked our waitress.

"Can I have the classic onion soup with melted gruyere for starters," I replied. I met eyes with my host. "And for my *main* meal, I'll have the sautéed pork medallions with the orange compare sauce."

"Merci, monsieur. And for you?"

"I'll try the couscous salad with the yogurt dressing for starters, and then for entrée—" He quickly poked his tongue out at me. "—the grilled chicken breast with the honey mustard glaze."

"Anything else, men?" she asked.

I shook my head.

"Baked potatoes on the side," Cameron replied.

"Merci, monsieur." She collected our menus and left us.

My charming date reached for my hand, so I slid it across the table. He began to rub my palm. "Nathan, you keep freaking out when I want to treat you. Why? I'm giving you the perfect vacation."

"Cameron, I feel like I'm using you. I have got some money. Can I make a deal with you?"

"What's the deal?"

"You can pay for dinners, but let me pay for shows and museums and things. What do you think? Hello. Do you have an answer?"

"Let me put it this way." He leaned forward. "No."

"Cameron!"

"Just hear me out. I'm spoiled rotten. Ever since my parents made money, I've been a boy blessed with everything I need in life. Sure, I try to get involved somehow in making my own money, but nothing has quite worked out. So my parents have no problem in looking after my finances. Nathan, what's that look on your face?"

"Continue. I'll reserve my comments until I hear your whole monologue."

"Okay, as I was saying, I'm spoiled. I have more money than I know what to do with, and as a gift to myself, I'd like to treat my heavenly Australian."

"I don't think 'heavenly' works either."

"Regardless, do you see my point, Nathan?"

"But can't you see you're buying my love?"

He stopped rubbing my hand in a way I was sure was accidental. "I don't mean to buy your love, but let's look at it from your perspective. I'm not judging, but the type of vacation I can give you in Manhattan is out of your means."

"For someone who wanted to know my perspective, you're definitely telling me what that perspective is." I sipped my cocktail.

"So, let me spoil you this week."

"But it makes me feel cheap. Cameron, I like you, but perhaps I like you too much to take advantage of you."

"But you're not."

"Let me ask you something. How well do you know your butler, Roger?"

"Very well."

"When's his birthday?"

"It's October. Or is it November? No, it's definitely October."

"What date in October?"

"Early October."

"Yes, Cameron, but what date?"

"I don't see what this has to do with our conversation."

"Okay, what did you buy for his last birthday?"

"An expensive bottle of gin. I had it flown in specially."

"And how did you celebrate with him?"

"I didn't."

"How did he celebrate?"

"I don't know."

"I see."

"What do you see, Nathan? He wanted to celebrate alone on the town."

"But he's your staff member. Didn't you take him out to dinner?"

"No, but I don't see what this has to do—"

"You're happy to take me to dinner and show me a good time, yet you hardly know me. But you haven't spoiled someone who lives in the same apartment as you."

Our entrées or starters or whatever they were, were served. As I thanked our waitress, I caught other patrons glancing away from our table and chaotically diving into their meals. My dining partner noticed too, and then sheepishly peered into his couscous.

"Looks like we're the floor show," I joked.

"That's what happens when you dine with an argumentative Australian."

Chapter Eight

WE SAID FEW words in the elevator as we made our way up to Cameron's apartment, but everywhere I looked I saw the mirrored reflection of two men on an unsuccessful date. We were a photographic portrait of an American finding solace in his cell phone with social media friends and an Australian trapped in a magnificent city with no affordable means of finding a welcoming hotel.

I thought we ascended way past his floor, trapped in a space where eye contact was not an option. He mumbled something about what a friend was up to. I said "That's nice" and looked away so I couldn't see us in the reflected surfaces. But everywhere I turned, another mirrored wall showed me the same story. A romance that was going nowhere.

I sighed in relief when we reached his floor. The doors slid open. He stepped out first. As he fished for his keys, he turned to me. "Nathan, would you feel more comfortable in the guest room?"

"I think that's your way of saying that you *want* me in the guest room."

"Don't second-guess me."

I heard a thud from inside his apartment, followed by a shriek. "What was that?" I asked.

"Oh, Rowena has been on the sauce again. And it's not even a full moon."

"Who's Rowena?"

He found his keys and promptly opened the door. In a miniskirt hardly bigger than a diaper lay Roger. Two oranges rolled out of his leopard-skin-print top and under the coffee table. His ginger wig looked like something that once climbed trees.

"You're home early, Cam darling," squealed Roger, or Rowena. "And who is this vision of beauty next to you?"

"Rowena, you've already met Nathan, the annoying Australian."

He, or she, picked themself off the floor with the grace of a stoned elephant. "Oh, so the date didn't go well."

"Why did you pick tonight of all nights to have a drink?"

"Darling, you told me to get a good night's sleep. So I opened the gin to help me rest. But then I was awakened from the inside, and my alter ego had to speak. Now, let me get you some cocktails."

"Roger, when's your birthday?" I asked.

"It's Rowena, dearie."

"Sorry. Rowena, when's your birthday?"

"In February. Why do you ask?"

I wore a shit-eating grin.

"Rowena, when is *Roger's* birthday?" asked Cameron.

"The fourth of October. Why this fascination with birthdays? Are we doing horoscopes?"

My failed date gave me a satisfied smirk. "No reason," he said.

The style-deprived transvestite flounced to the kitchen and poured gin and ginger beer into two large glasses before topping them with ice. She wandered back, passed us our drinks, and then grabbed an arm from both of us. We crashed into the modular lounge as she pulled us downward, landing herself in the middle. A little of my cocktail spilled on my jeans.

"Now then, Cam dearie, were you treating this gorgeous man like a plaything?"

"Rowie, I was showing him some hospitality."

"And you, our little koala bear, were you not appreciative of Cam's generosity?"

"Koala bear?"

"Just work with me, dearie."

"Why were you on the floor when we walked in?"

"You *are* an annoying Australian, aren't you?" She winked. "I was channeling my inner diva by dancing on the coffee table. I tell you, heels will be the death of me."

"Rowie, is this conversation going anywhere?" Cameron asked.

"When have you ever known me to steer you wrong, my faithful employer?" She held our hands in her lap, a little too close to her private parts. "Now, Nathan, why not appreciate an all-expenses-paid trip to Manhattan? Why, it's what every impressionable young girl dreams of."

"But if this relationship has any chance of working, it has to be a two-way street."

Chapter Nine

ON MY FOURTH day in New York, we had lunch in a chic burger joint. Fumes from the grill were tapping me on the shoulder, demanding to be noticed. Sizzling bacon, farm-fresh eggs, and cheese that spread itself like a lap dancer all over my crisp beef patty oozed out of a toasted bun. And the sauce! Oh, the sauce.

"Nathan, you're eyeing off that hamburger as if you've never seen one before."

"We have gourmet burgers in Sydney, but there's something authentic about having one in America. Plus, this is the cheapest meal we've had since we've been here. Can I pay the bill, I mean, the check?"

"I paid at the counter when we ordered. Remember?"

"Oh yes. I forgot. There's something about good food that alters my perception."

"I'm glad you like it. Now, how do you feel about a Broadway show tonight?"

"Another, Cameron? That's the third one. You're spending way too much."

"Not this conversation again." He frowned, then bit into his grilled chicken sandwich. He looked away to the other patrons. So did I.

College-aged students mixed conversation and social media, sharing images as they passed around their phones. A middle-aged couple in tacky shirts sat staring at each other with nothing to say. An upsized family were stacking their plates with enough food to feed a small kingdom, yet they made a point of sipping diet cola. And other funky inner-city types enjoyed fries and gossip while taking turns checking out the other customers.

"Cameron, tell me something about yourself."

"What do you need to know?"

"Well, every time we talk, you tell me about Roger or about friends I haven't met yet, and because I haven't met them, I feel like I'm listening to the plot of a soap opera. And we've talked about movies and books and sometimes celebrities. Or you've told me what you've got planned for me the next day. But you don't really open up about yourself. I still feel I don't know what makes you tick."

He threw his hands in the air. "Okay, what do you want to know?"

"Your parents. Every time I ask about them, you don't say much."

"You haven't said much about your parents, either."

"You haven't asked."

"Well, Nathan, I'm asking."

"My parents are humble. They live out of Sydney in a mini-city called Newcastle. They worked hard to bring me and my sister up, and they shared a lot of love with us. My dad's a carpenter and my mum does admin work. And to me, they're the best parents in the world."

"Why did you leave Newcastle?"

"To start making my fortune, and even though it hasn't happened yet, it will."

He smiled. "Yeah, a lot of people come to Manhattan to make their fortune."

"I think it's the lure of big cities. Yet somehow people born in those cities don't really see the opportunities around them."

"Hmm." He dipped a fry into our small container of mustard. "Do you see them much?"

"My parents? This is the thing. On one hand, I'm trying not to visit too often because I want to be independent. After all, it was my decision to move to Sydney. Yet too often I miss them. So I travel home and help Dad with odd jobs around the house. Mum always says I'm losing weight, but I assure her I'm eating well. I mean, I get freebies at Lucy's café. You know what mothers are like."

"Yeah, my mom asks the same. You'd think it's illegal to like someone else's cooking better than hers." He sipped his raspberry soda. I sat waiting for more information about his family. Eventually I watched the cars zip past the window. And every night at dinner, I'd wait for some tidbit about his background. Who were his past lovers? How did his mum, or mom in his case, and dad make their millions? And did he ever hold down a job? But I never pried. Instead, I studied his adorable eyes cloaked in their designer frames. I lost myself in lips softer than butter. Perhaps this was enough for him? Perhaps, as I knew all along, this was merely a short affair?

Chapter Ten

CHEAP CHINESE WAS the choice of the night, as Ben and Lucy took me out for a gossip session. A mix of exotic sauces dripped off roasted sliced duck, bite-sized beef, and succulent chicken. Chopsticks brought the aroma closer to our lips. At first, some savory sensation would explode in my mouth before rice subdued the taste like a dance, back and forth.

"Nathan, it's chicken for goodness sake," said Lucy. "You know, chicken? You can fry it. You can roast it. You can poach it. It's not some weird thing you've never tried before."

"I agree with Lucy," Ben added. "The way you're slobbering over your meal, you'd swear you had no sex for the past week."

The corners of my mouth stretched back like an archer's bow.

"Oh, you did have sex!"

"And it just got better and better as the week wore on," I replied.

"So, is there a future with Cameron?" Lucy asked.

"Who cares?" said Ben. "I want to know more about the sex. Is he a top or bottom?"

"Let's just say, ladies, our chemistry works."

"So there is a future," Lucy concluded.

"I'm not sure. I mean, we had a good time and everything, but I'm not sure how I feel."

My friends shared a glance before rolling their eyes.

"You guys are as subtle as dynamite."

"We know you better than you think," said Ben. "We've seen this before."

Lucy raised her palm like a policeman stopping traffic. "Nathan, why aren't you sure how you feel?"

I put down my chopsticks. "Look, I had a great time. It was a magical romance for a week, but reality hit us both on the last night. He threw a party in my honor so I could meet his friends. Rowena was mixing drinks—"

"Who's Rowena?" asked Ben.

"I'll get to that."

"SO, WE'VE HAD more meals in the last week than there are days in a month," I said. "We even had soul food in Harlem. I've never had soul food before." I started counting all our dates on my fingers as I spoke. "Plus you've taken me to three Broadway shows, the Sex Museum, the Guggenheim, Central Park, that battleship with all the military planes, various clubs and bars, and now a farewell party!"

"I had Roger plan the party," Cameron confessed. "I didn't want to spend time away from you."

A very trendy crowd murmured in our midst. Roger, who had switched to his alter ego several hours into the celebration, made sure the endless cocktails were more vibrant than the colors you'd find in a kaleidoscope. Even a band, who looked like they stepped out of a retro beach movie, played surf tunes to keep our hips swinging.

Both Cameron and I had Hawaiian shirts to wear, while Rowena sported a tie-dyed sarong and an afro wig. And around us, interesting guests wore chic little skirts, James Dean–style jackets, hippie gear, and mod wear.

"You haven't introduced me yet," said a middle-aged woman to Cameron. Her rust-colored coat had a masculine cut. Yet she elegantly held a long-stemmed cigarette holder with something that smelled very much like a joint burning on the end.

"Sorry," said my charming American. "This is my friend, Nathan. And this well-dressed lady is my aunt Beverley."

"Nice to meet you," I said.

She took my hand and kissed it. "I hope you don't think me too forward; it's just that you've got such fascinating features."

"My aunt likes to flirt."

"It runs in the family," she replied. She gave me a measured wink. "Now, nephew, where have you been hiding this handsome Englishman?"

"I'm Australian."

"It's your accent. I never can tell the difference."

"I need you!" yelled a girl in a flower necklace. She was the drummer of the band and was addressing our host.

"It's time," Cameron said.

"Time for what?" I asked.

He kissed me on the cheek and then headed for the microphone stand.

"You're in for a treat," whispered Aunt Beverley, her voice raspy from years of smoking.

"He sings?" I asked.

"He sings," she replied.

A laid-back strum of the bass guitar started the song, followed by a drum beat. Then the vocal. And before I knew it, I was being serenaded in front of a room full of acquaintances. But, wow! What a unique experience.

"I've never seen him go out on a limb for someone like this before," said his aunt.

I smiled politely, then closed my eyes. He was crooning. His honey voice made my soul rise out of my body and search for a dream. And in the hip nightclub that appeared in my mind, he wore a gray suit with a crimson tie, standing tall in front of the trumpet section who were waiting for their cue. And I was the only one in the club.

"Where are you?" asked Aunt Beverley in a low tone.

I wanted to say I was in love but stopped myself. I realized it was rude to have my eyes closed during Cam's song. I opened them. He had me in his sights. I wanted to jump into the waves on his Hawaiian shirt and end up on a deserted island with just him and me.

"Would you like a toke of my cigarette, Nathan?"

"No, thank you. I think the fumes have already hit me."

"He's quite a catch, my nephew. And it's so unlike him to spoil anyone like he's been spoiling you."

"You know about our week together?"

"Roger has been talking about nothing else, tonight." She spoke into my ear. "Do you like my nephew?"

"I think he's a very special guy."

"Not quite what I meant, Nathan. Do you *like* him?" The small gathering stepped closer to the band. Cameron was now humming as if forgetting the words to a lullaby. "Your hesitancy to answer worries me, Nathan."

"Beverley, I like him. This is all new to me. I mean, we've spent a lot of time with each other, but I still need to know how *I* feel."

"Just don't break his heart."

People applauded. I knew my bewilderment was showing on my face, so I smiled, yet I felt like a mime with a mask. Cameron raised a brow. I clapped as the other guests studied me. They were smiling back. My disguise must have worked on them.

He came to me, and as I briefly turned to his aunt, I was surprised to find she wasn't there. "What did you think?" he asked.

I wrapped my arms around his broad shoulders and hugged him as if he was something keeping me afloat at sea. "Your aunt is as direct as a lesbian." I spoke right into his ear.

"That's because she is a lesbian."

We moved apart. "Of course. Why didn't I pick up on it?"

"What did she say?"

"She's looking after your interests, that's all."

"Sorry if she was too direct, but that's why I like her."

"That's funny. You don't like *me* when I'm direct."

"I'll get used to it, Nathan." He seemed puzzled. "You know, I just asked you what you thought of my serenade, yet you began talking about my aunt."

"Sorry, it's just that she leaves an impression."

"And my singing didn't?"

"Cameron, your song was the most romantic gesture any lover has ever treated me with."

We hugged again, but after a short while, he asked, "So what did my aunt say?"

"Nothing, really. She just asked me how I felt."

"And what did you say?"

"I said it's early in our relationship, and I'm still finding how I fit in."

He pulled away. "You said that?"

"No, actually I didn't. That just came out then."

"Nathan, I just sang to you. You told me it was the most romantic gesture anyone has ever done for you. For goodness sake, I'm trying my hardest to make you feel like you fit in."

"My charming American, this has been a whirlwind week. We've been up every night so my body clock knows where it stands when I return to Sydney. And you've spoiled me rotten with early morning tours of your city. We've made love in the afternoon before sleeping, then had dinner for breakfast at some of the most wonderful restaurants."

"I'm not sure if I like where this is heading."

"Cameron, let's get real. We've only spent a week together. How does anyone know how they feel in a week?"

"YOU SAID THAT?" Lucy stared at me like an alien life form.

"I was being honest," I replied.

"Nathan, honesty isn't one of your most endearing features," said Ben.

"Well, I didn't want to lead him on. Besides, he's spoilt. Not in a spoilt brat way, but in a way where he can have anything he wants whenever he wants. What if I'm just his latest fad?"

"Nathan's right. He's had his fun in New York with Cameron. He should go and find a rich man in Barcelona. Or maybe San Francisco."

Lucy hit him with her chopsticks. "Romance is lost on both of you," she said. She rested her finger on her chin. "This is about Elliot, isn't it?"

"How did we get onto the subject of Elliot?" I asked. They both stared at me. "Elliot is ancient history. Seriously, he is."

"But you still haven't let him go."

"I'm not going to live *your* fairy-tale romance."

"See, this is what he does all the time," claimed Ben. "He changes the subject when we talk about Elliot."

"Nate, darling, you've been single for a year and a half," said Lucy. "You have to move on."

I sighed.

"You have a man who is the fantasy of most single women—rich, handsome, lovable."

I could feel my eyes tear up.

"Spoil yourself. Get lost in his world. See where he takes you. If he's not your final destiny, his love might prepare you for the man who is."

Ben handed me his napkin.

I wiped my cheeks. A lion roared. I picked up my phone and through blurred eyes read the text.

"You look lost," said Ben. "Who's the message from?"

"It's Cam's butler and his aunt," I replied. "They're in Sydney!"

Chapter Eleven

ROGER WAS IN Rowena mode with a tatty blonde wig and a bridal dress. Aunt Beverley was also in white, but her outfit consisted of a jumpsuit and blue suede shoes. And both had bags the size of luggage under their eyes.

"This is how you travel?" I asked.

"I wanted to parade my outfit for you Australians," Rowena replied, rotating her hand above her head as she said this.

"I take it you're Dolly Parton?"

"No, dear Nathan. I'm Priscilla Presley."

"When was Priscilla blonde?"

"Sweetheart, all gals go blonde once in their lives."

"Huh?"

Aunt Beverley took my hand and lowered her face to meet mine. "Autistic for Elvis," she said.

"What?"

"It's the charity we ran out of to jump on a plane to see you."

"You didn't think to go home and change first?"

"We couldn't," Rowena replied. "Cameron rang us in drunken tears, which is how we got your number."

"I was wondering about that."

"Remember this, Nate. Whenever he's drunk, you can ask Cam anything without him remembering the next day." She winked like a mistress who knew all the tricks.

"So you left the fundraiser and boarded a plane to see me?"

"Of course. We had to visit the root of Cam's problem."

"Thanks. Were you both drunk when you made that decision?"

"Yes, but an eighteen-hour flight sobers you up, no matter how much gin you drink."

I gazed at the dynamic duo with their oversized cocktails. It was good to see them continue their party down under, as the other patrons in this gay pub didn't bat an eyelid at their appearance. The music pulsated, and Rowena's oversized ass swung back and forth like an out-of-control wrecking ball.

"No time for that, love," Beverley insisted. "We have to talk some sense into Nathan."

A mustached man grabbed a chunk of Rowena's swaying behind, and she purred. But Aunt Bev gave a look that could curdle milk, and her admirer slipped away quietly.

"Okay, what do you need to say to me?" I asked.

"Why do you think *we* need to do all the talking?" Bev replied.

"Because I don't know what to say. And what I had to say, I said to Cameron."

"And he said it back to us in a drunken stupor over the phone, just when I was about to begin my rendition of 'Devil in Disguise.'"

Something unnerved me about the way she said that song title.

"Nate, dear, how do you feel about Cam?" Rowena asked. Her eyelids fluttered when she mentioned her employer's name.

"I like him."

"And?"

"And I like him."

"And he likes you. So what's the problem?"

Aunt Beverley leaned forward as Rowena tried to look serious. And somehow, having the ghost of Elvis and a bad Priscilla look-a-like judge me made me feel less threatened. "I don't know him."

"What!" Rowena's head flicked back so fast that her wig flew into someone's beer. Fortunately, the patron was too drunk to notice. She then turned, scrunched her face, and looked me right in the eye. "He paraded you all around New York, showing you the sights and—"

Bev put a finger to Rowena's lips. "How much does he know about you?" Bev asked.

"A fair bit. More than I know about him."

"But what about—" Rowena began.

"My nephew lives like an only child. He always has. He always will."

"Then you get what I'm saying, Beverley?"

"But the point is, that's him. He doesn't know any better."

"And that's hard for me to take."

"Why, Nathan? In his only child way, he's showing that he loves you."

"Does he love me?"

They exchanged glances before Rowena rested her hairy hand on my shoulder. "Nate, dear," she said, "you should've heard him crying over the phone."

"Why? Because I was a toy he couldn't have?"

"You're quite bitter for a young man," Aunt Beverley noted.

"He is, isn't he?" Rowena agreed. "I'd say Nate was in love once and obviously had his heart broken."

"And if I know the weaker sex the way I do, I'd say he still is in love."

I looked into the small crowd, more for a sense of safety than anything else. It was late and anyone who began their flirting early would already be at home working their one-night stand. All that was left were the vultures, drinking heavily for courage while fawning over their prey. And in this desperate dance, I saw nothing of my own experience.

For I knew the look of love. I knew what it felt like when I wore it on my own face. Elliot was my king, my queen, my emperor, my man. And I could rely on his loving gaze when I shut the door on the world.

In the far corner, I saw someone with a shirt similar to mine. He rested his hand behind his lover's neck as he searched for his partner's soul with penetrating eyes. It was a look of infatuation. A look that was the start of something more.

"That's how Cameron looks at you."

"I know, Rowena," I said. "I'm seeing how others see me and Cam."

"So who's the other man?" Beverley asked. "The one you can't forget?"

I stayed focused on the bewitching couple. "Maybe it doesn't matter. Maybe after all is said and done, it doesn't matter anymore."

A lion roared. I fished my phone out of my pocket. I read the text.

"Why are you looking at us like that?" Rowena asked.

"Yes, Nathan, what's the matter?"

"Did you know about this?" I asked.

"About what?"

"Cameron's in Sydney."

Rowena's hands fluttered like the wings of a bird caught in a fishing net.

Bev snatched my phone and read the text for herself.

"Don't tell him we're here," the cross-dresser cried. "He'll think we're meddling."

"Sweethearts, you *are* meddling!"

Rowena's hands fluttered even more as Aunt Beverley slowly handed me my phone.

I didn't take it. Instead, I opened my arms wide and embraced them, bringing my mouth to their ears. "But you know what? I'm glad you're meddling."

Chapter Twelve

I VIEWED THE harbor from his hotel room. Ferries glided like ice skaters on the water as seagulls assessed the passengers on their lit decks. The Museum of Contemporary Art stood as a Rubik's Cube bent out of shape, clinging to its former self. And the Opera House sat to the side like a collection of dazzling seashells a child had left behind.

"You live in a beautiful city, Nathan." He sat on the edge of the bed, peering through his designer eyewear at the view.

"What made you come to Sydney, Cameron?"

"I'm not one for unfinished business."

I smiled to myself. "Does Roger know you're here?"

"No. But when he works it out, he'll drink all the gin and dress in a kaftan or something."

"You really need to find someone to give him makeup tips."

"I asked Aunt Beverley once, but she glared at me like a restless corpse and reminded me that she never wore the stuff."

I giggled as I turned to him. "I'm sorry about our last night in New York."

"Why?"

"You really need to ask?"

"Nathan, I think I know why you're apologizing." He patted the bedspread next to him. "But I want to hear it from you."

I sat. "My charming American, I took you for granted. I think that's why I'm apologizing. Perhaps if you were just a friend spoiling me, I'd appreciate what you're doing. But you want to be more, and I feel really odd being second fiddle."

"Second fiddle? What are you talking about?"

"I can never spoil you the way you're spoiling me, and it just feels wrong."

"But I'm wooing you."

"No, you're not!" Those words came out with more force than I intended. "You're winning me over, and it feels odd."

He scrunched his curved pink lips. "My little Nate, I don't know any other way to woo someone I like. And it's not so bad, is it? My parents still shower me with presents, even at my age."

"And what was the last present they gave you?" He looked out the window. "See, you don't remember."

"So what? It's the gesture that counts."

"But what good are gestures if they're not remembered?"

"Didn't you like the places I took you?"

"I loved them, Cameron, but that's not my point. Madonna said in a song—"

"What? We're quoting Madonna now?"

"Hear me out. She sang that long-stem roses are a way to someone's heart. But they need to show you how they feel through the love they make, not through the presents they give you."

"I thought we had great sex. You moaned and gasped like you were having a religious experience."

"Cam, you're good in bed. You have techniques that could make a gigolo blush. But we haven't made love."

"Love?" He gazed at the ceiling. "I showed you my world, Nathan. Isn't that love?"

I stood and began to pace. "I know you're rich. I know your parents are self-made millionaires. At least, I think they're millionaires." He nodded. "You have a close relationship with your butler. You spend your days dining and doing other things. Actually, I'm not sure what you do with your time except for showing up in Prague on a whim. Or Sydney, for that matter. And I know you can sing. But, Cameron, who are *you*?"

"You know who I am. I'm that charming American."

"But I don't know your childhood dramas. I don't know what your goals are. I don't know what makes you cry. I don't know what scares you. Hell, I don't even know what your parents are like."

"You've met my aunt."

"Yeah, but your parents are a mystery. In the week we spent together, you didn't say much about them."

"Okay, Nate. I promise you'll meet them soon."

"But that's still not my point, Cam. To me, you're a charming American who is in a hurry to woo me and call me his boyfriend. Yet all you know about me is that I'm more of a realist than you." I stopped pacing. "I need to be let inside and to see the world through your beautiful brown eyes. Not just inhabit your world with you."

A pair of voices, one male, one female, debated the price of their room as they made their way down the hall outside. The ding of the elevator sounded, and a robotic voice pronounced which floor they were on.

And through this fuss, Cameron gazed at me like a boy who'd been reprimanded. I licked my bottom lip, which tasted as if salt had been smeared on it. I swallowed.

He stood and took small steps toward me, staring at me with a politician's poker face. He closed his eyelids like shutters drawn slowly by lovers. He reached for my waist and held me against him, then gently caressed the back of my scalp, easing my head to rest on his chest.

He clasped his hand in mine, as we rocked back and forth like an old couple waltzing. He sang his serenade song from the party, but slower, as if the night had no end.

He smelled like a laundered shirt. Crisp and clean, yet waiting to be soiled. I sank deeper into him, if that was at all possible. He wasn't my rich admirer out to spoil me. He was no New York regular known at countless restaurants. He was simply Cameron, a man who had a past, and I could feel it through his embrace, finally ready to be exposed a little at a time.

Chapter Thirteen

"I'M IN AWE of you," said Cam.

"Why?" I mumbled.

"I didn't think you were awake."

"I can feel your body tossing and turning. You're in the wrong time zone."

Lights from Circular Quay still peeped through the balcony window, into the underplayed drama that was our lives. But I could also sense the first rays of daylight on my pillow.

"Do you always tell me that you're in awe of me when I'm asleep?" I sat up.

He looked like a teenager who'd been caught masturbating by his mother.

"What are you embarrassed about?"

"I must seem rich and shallow to you, Nate."

I held him. "My charming Cameron, that's the last thing I think when I'm with you. Hey, a shallow person doesn't serenade me in front of his house guests."

He laughed softly.

"But I know you have brooding secrets, and underneath the surface, I'm determined to find out more about you."

"My parents won a bit of money in a lottery, then Dad bought a business that couldn't fail."

"Go on." I let go of my caring man and sat up again.

He clenched his lips for a moment. "My dad bought a funeral home."

"So why didn't you tell me that in New York?"

"I didn't want you to think we were the Addams Family."

"Do you have a cousin with overgrown hair?"

"No."

"Did your mum, sorry, mom feed a carnivorous plant with an Egyptian name?"

"No."

"Did you have an uncle who came in handy during electrical blackouts?"

"I see your point, Nate. It's just that it's a morbid profession. I didn't know how to tell you."

"So, how young were you when you saw your first corpse?"

"Too young. Our home was upstairs from the business because we couldn't afford a separate apartment, and one Christmas morning, I tiptoed downstairs to look for presents."

"Huh? They weren't under the Christmas tree?"

"No one else was up. So in my kid-like logic, I thought there might also be presents downstairs, and I wouldn't get in trouble if I opened one of them instead of the ones under the tree."

"Yeah, kids will always find a way to justify their actions."

"So, I turned the doorknob and was surprised it was unlocked. Dad was down there and freaked out when he saw me. He told me to get back into bed straightaway. I thought Santa might still be around and I'd get to see him. So I ran past my dad and saw a woman lying on a stretcher." He smiled gently. "She was about the age of my mom, and in my mind, I couldn't work out why my dad was upset that I'd seen him with this sleeping woman."

"Go on, Cam. I'm intrigued."

"So, Dad calmed down and told me she was Sleeping Beauty, and he was staying up to let Prince Charming through the door when he got here."

"That's kind of sweet. Morbid, but sweet."

"I wanted to stay and wait for Prince Charming with him, but my dad said I could open one present if I went upstairs, as long as I then went straight to bed. I did."

I wrapped my arm around him. "So how did your parents become millionaires?"

"They branched out. There were times when I wouldn't see my dad for months because he'd open a new funeral home somewhere interstate, while Mom ran our home business with Aunt Beverley."

I couldn't help myself. I began laughing. Cam watched as, little by little, his own chuckling sounded like someone starting a car. Then we were both giggling wildly.

"I can see your Aunt Beverley with the dead. She'd scare them more than they'd scare her."

"The comments she made about some of the men that came in had my mom in stitches. But I was too young to understand."

"How did your parents cope living above all those corpses?"

"When I was a teenager, Dad told me they had plenty of sex to take their minds off what was downstairs. That and a lot of after-work cocktails. Come to think of it, they still drink lots of cocktails."

I wiped my eyes and took a few deep breaths. Cam grinned like a Cheshire cat. "So when did you stop living above the dead?"

"When I was fifteen. By then we had enough staff to run the many funeral homes around the country."

"Cam, let me assure you, you're pretty normal for someone who's grown up around cadavers."

"Thank you, Nate. I actually appreciate you saying that to me."

I snuck a kiss. "So why are you in awe of me?"

He peered at the view. The sky's pink hue had met the ocean. Seagulls watched the first sleepy commuters making their way into the city by ferry. And the calm of this scene was reflected on the face of this charming man.

"Yes, why am I in awe of you, Nate?" He held my hand. "Maybe it's because you're not embarrassed about your past. Or maybe because less is expected of you."

Chapter Fourteen

"It's NOTHING FLASH, but it's home," I said, jiggling my key in the lock.

"Nate, you found the skeletons in my closet early this morning. Now it's my turn to explore some more of yours."

The door opened on my messy front room. "Excuse the laundry on the floor. It's to remind me to fold it. I was going to do it last night before bed, but then you texted me."

"It's your home. Don't apologize for being you." He kissed me before we stepped through the doorway. As we entered, he scanned the living room.

"You look sentimental, Cam."

"I grew up in a place this small." He clasped a hand over his mouth as fast as a snapping bear trap. "Sorry, that didn't come out the way I meant it."

"Don't apologize. It's what you wanted to say. Don't censor yourself." I headed for the kitchen. "Can I get you a drink?"

"Do you have a club soda?"

"You know, I've heard that expression in American TV shows, but I don't actually know what a club soda is."

"It's basically just sparkling water."

"That I can do." I poured two glasses and returned to the lounge area. We toasted the magic night we just had. "So, what do you think of my humble home?"

"It's my enchanted younger years before the pretense of gay city life took over."

"I don't think your New York life is pretentious."

"That's not what I meant." He pointed to the stove, walking toward it. "There's a hot plate that has cooked hundreds of meals."

"Not by me. I eat at Lucy's café most of the time."

"True, but before you. Maybe a Polish migrant made dumplings most nights on that cooker. A Chinese woman might have stir-fried her socks off after that. This stove has a history well before you ignored it."

"Cam, it's just a stove."

"By the time I left childhood far behind, I didn't have just a stove. I had staff to cook. And my mom kept renovating her kitchen more times than an obsessive-compulsive washes his hands." He opened my utensil drawer and pulled out my potato masher. "See this! When I was a boy, this was a rocket ship." He grabbed my ice cream scooper and raised it above his head, while making the masher fly toward it. "Space Station Zebra to Rocket Ship Beta, can you hear me?"

"Isn't the ice cream scoop too small to be a space station?"

"Nate, stop overthinking and pick up the cheese grater."

I did, holding it close to the ice-cream scoop.

"Alien space ship in our midst. Zebra, fly in for a closer look."

"We are from the planet Beacon," I said, sounding like a geriatric Kermit the Frog. "We are not here to judge you, Earthlings. We are here to learn your culture."

"And we welcome the chance to learn about you, Beacon-lings. But you look like you have sharp mounds on your ship. You could cut us to shreds. Should we proceed with caution?"

"We may have pointy bits, but they are not lethal."

"Do you Beacon-lings need that much protection?"

"In time, we'll let our guard down. The more we learn about you Earthlings, the more we will trust you."

"We are ready to be an open book for you to study from."

I saw my smile reflected in his glasses. Slowly we placed the utensils on the kitchen bench. I breathed him in, hearing him let a breath out. We kissed. I felt myself falling. I was somewhere in deep space, exploring without my shields up.

Who is this? My replacement? I ignored Elliot's voice in my head. *I can tell by the way you're holding him he's not just a one-nighter.*

"What's the matter, Nate?" my charming American asked.

"What makes you think something's the matter?"

"You just tensed up."

Looks like I'm still number one.

"Nothing's the matter, Cam. I just got distracted."

"Am I still moving too fast for you?"

"No!" I clutched him tighter. "This is the right pace for me, Cam. I'm loving how our relationship is going, Cam. I'm falling—"

You're falling! growled Elliot. *I'm gone for a nanosecond, and you're shagging other men. What's wrong with having sex with me, for old time's sake?*

"You're falling?" asked my gentle New Yorker. "Why did you stop midsentence?" He had a smile as wide as a boy's at an amusement park.

"I'm falling for a man from another city," I said, saying this to both of them.

"So am I," Cam replied.

I kissed his lips hard, never opening my mouth. And I held him like an old friend. But then, Elliot began to weep.

He wasn't loud, but I couldn't ignore him. It was the whimper of a pet that had been forgotten, not knowing his place in my life. He was a pet I no longer wanted to feed or take for walks. But I didn't want to take him to a shelter or get him put to sleep. Somehow I just wanted him in the corner, loyal and quiet.

"Why are you crying, Nathan?" Cameron asked.

"Am I?" I wiped my tears with the back of my hands. "I'm just getting overemotional."

"Be honest with me. Did I do something wrong?"

He gazed at me like a parent with a sick child. Then he wrapped his arms around me and waited for a response, searching me with his thoughtful brown eyes. And over his shoulder, I saw Elliot, his arms crossed and foot tapping.

He's doing everything wrong.

"Who are you looking at, Nate?" Cameron glanced over his shoulder, then back to me. I stared into his eyes, determined not to look away.

I held you closer and for longer than that weird guy with an accent. And what is he doing on my territory? We still have a connection, Nathan. You know we do. Elliot unfolded his arms and took a step toward me. *We have a bond that can never be broken.* He took another step, then another until he stood right behind Cameron. *You belong to me, Nathan. You always have.*

"Let go of me!" I screamed.

My loving American jumped back as if lightning struck. He looked through me as if I wasn't there. The odd thing was, Elliot was the one no longer there.

"I wasn't yelling at you, Cameron."

"But I'm the only other person here, and I really thought we broke down some barriers last night."

"I have something to tell you, and I really don't know how to put it into words."

"I would never shout at you, Nathan, the way you just did."

"It wasn't at you, I promise."

"What did I do wrong?"

"Cameron, you're not listening. I didn't yell at you."

"I'm going back to my hotel."

"No, please don't. This is my day to spoil you."

He scratched his head endlessly. "I want you to know something, Nate. I'd never yell at anyone the way you just yelled at me. I felt like a mutt you didn't want anymore." He headed toward my front door.

"Cameron, you're laboring your point. Why aren't you giving me a chance to explain myself?"

"I'm going."

"No, seriously, wait!"

He huffed. "Nathan, you've taken your time to warm to me, and just when I think we've connected, you start acting weird. I can read between the lines. You don't feel the same way about me as I do about you. So, I've put you in the position where you've been too nice to hurt my feelings. And too nice to be honest with yourself."

"No, Cameron, that's not it!"

"The simple truth is, I'm more into you than you are into me. And that's nothing to hide. It's best I cut my losses before I get too involved."

I tried to grab his arm and stop him from running away, but he nudged me aside. As the door shut hard, Elliot's satisfied laughter echoed in my ears.

Chapter Fifteen

"WHY ARE YOU at work?" Lucy asked.

"Because Cam went back home," I replied.

It was late afternoon, and I hadn't been rostered. But I needed something to distract me from my over-ticking mind.

"Nathan, your foot is tapping like a jackhammer. You're in no state to work."

"Yes, I am. Just watch." I turned to a patron sitting by herself at the nearest table. "Have you ordered, madam?"

"I was just about to pay the bill," she replied.

"Then I should get you something to take home." She shook her head, but I headed for a jar of white chocolate and macadamia cookies near the till. "You'll love these. Lucy bakes them herself."

The jar slipped like a fortune from my hands, scattering crumbs and glass shards when it crashed to the floor. The customer gave me a sheepish grin.

"Nathan, come to my office," said Lucy. "Taylor, sorry to ask you, but could you please clean up?"

My fellow employee headed for the broom cupboard as I followed Lucy. She offered me a seat, but I didn't feel like sitting. With her hands clutched in her lap, she listened.

"Okay, I had a little accident, but I'm fit to work. Really, I am."

"Nathan, how many customers are in my café at the moment?"

"Well, there's that girl who needed a cookie."

"And who else?"

I stared blankly.

"You don't know, do you? There's a couple with young children, two teenagers who should be at school, and that old man who only comes in for coffee as he reads."

"*That* many people? See, you need me here."

"Nathan, my point is, you're so preoccupied about the reason Cameron has gone back to New York that you don't know what's going on around you. And seriously, that old man is the one you talk to all the time, and you didn't realize he was there."

"Felix is here in the café?"

"Yep, and you didn't notice him. He was watching you frantically giving away my stock to that woman for free."

I lowered my head.

"Nathan, sit down, please."

I did.

"Now, when did you last see Cameron?"

"At the airport."

"Go on."

"I rang and rang him constantly for a proper goodbye."

"Why was he going to leave without saying goodbye?"

"And he finally told me when his flight was."

"I guess we'll get to why he was leaving eventually."

"I texted him. He told me he was in line in security, and there was no use coming to the airport, but I did anyway. You know something, Lucy? He wasn't going through security. He was in line getting his boarding pass. I wanted to run up to him and talk, but I felt betrayed. He obviously didn't want to see me, so I stood watching him. He checked the time. He sipped coffee from a paper cup. He took his passport out from a zip in his luggage."

"Didn't he see you?"

"No, I watched from a distance."

"Why was he leaving without saying goodbye?"

A lump formed in my throat "Lucy, Elliot won't leave me alone."

"But he's been dead for eighteen months."

"I know. He haunts me, Lucy. He just shows up when he feels like it."

She handed me a tissue from the box on her desk. Then another and another. She wrapped her arms around me tight. I gasped.

"There, there, friend. Let it out. Let it all out. His death was a tragedy, and Ben and I know that it's been hard for you."

"Why did Elliot have to leave me? We were so good together. He completed me."

At this point, Taylor entered her office. "Is everything all right, Lucy?"

"Everything is fine, but I'm going to leave you in charge for the rest of the evening, if you can extend your shift."

"No worries. I'll shut your door if you don't mind. Felix is asking about Nathan." He placed his hand on my shoulder momentarily before leaving.

"Nathan, Elliot didn't leave you willingly. That car veered into him as he was driving home to you. He loved you. We could all see that. You two were inseparable, and boy, the way he looked at you whenever you spoke, well, all I can say is that one day I want to find a love that deep."

"He's become nasty." I pulled away from her embrace and looked her in the eyes. "I don't know why. I mean, he was so loving when he was alive, but he's become mean and nasty and vicious."

Her eyes darted away. "My dear friend, have you been resting properly? Are you still jetlagged from your New York trip?"

"Lucy, he didn't show up at my place until two months ago. That was the time you were seeing Craig. He came to tell me that Craig was cheating on you." She looked at me. "He told me that Craig was seeing someone named Susan, and he wanted me to tell you."

"Nathan, how did you know he cheated on me? I never told you that. I was too embarrassed to tell anyone."

"Elliot told me to tell you that you are a good person. That you're worth loving and that Craig was not good enough for you. And that getting that silly tattoo done on his butt cheek was no reason to stay with him."

"I thought it was cute."

"What was the tattoo?"

"A heart."

"Did it have your name inside it?"

"No, it was just a red heart."

"In gay circles, a red heart on your butt might be an invitation."

She smirked. "Nathan, I never told you or Ben that he cheated on me because I still find it hard to let go. Or maybe I was too embarrassed that I was cheated on by someone I really loved. We both have past loves that have left their mark."

"While Ben is overdue for a real boyfriend that will take his breath away."

Lucy held me again, and I felt an invincible version of myself lurking somewhere deep inside. He was carefully assessing the situation, considering how to deal with Elliot.

"I don't want to see you lose Cameron."

"Lucy, he's not the love of my life."

"But you can't stay trapped in the past."

"Cameron is not Elliot. He's a flight of fancy. A dreamer."

"And he's a charming dreamer who likes you. Take a chance. Roll that dice. With everything you've tried to deal with since Elliot's death, now is the time to reward yourself with romance."

"A fairy-tale romance."

"You don't know that. And how will you know unless you give it a chance?"

"Lucy, for goodness sake, he's a rich idealist with more time to spare than a prison inmate."

"And you're punishing him."

"What have I got to punish him for?"

"For not being Elliot."

Chapter Sixteen

"WE NEED TO talk," I said.

Elliot looked up from the magazine he was flicking through. "I'll say we need to talk. Who is that joker with a kink for kitchen utensils?"

"That joker is my friend, Cameron."

"From what I saw the other day, he's more than a friend, Nathan."

I felt a mini volcano about to erupt inside me. "Elliot, you're dead!"

"That doesn't mean I'm not concerned about your welfare, lover."

"You are not my lover."

"But I was." A tear dripped down his cheek. I swallowed hard. That mini volcano disappeared without a trace.

"Elliot, you always will be my one true love, but..." I started gasping for breath before everything faded to black. When I woke, my private ghost was sitting next to me with his legs crossed.

"I was worried about you, Nathan. You don't usually pass out."

"You are not real, Elliot. You died eighteen months ago. You are *not* real."

"Then why am I talking to you?"

"Why don't you leave me alone? I buried you."

"Come now, Nathan, you know you can never say goodbye to me."

I ran to the kitchen and poured a glass of water from the tap. It flooded my throat, almost choking me. I poured another and drank again. I wiped my eyes and noticed Elliot standing just outside the kitchen.

"Why are you haunting me?"

"Because this is the only place I feel happy."

"Why? Isn't there a party in heaven that's boring without you?"

"This is the only place where I feel needed."

"What makes you think you're needed here?"

"I know I'm still needed here. The problem is, I'm not wanted anymore."

"Aren't they kind of the same thing?"

"Nathan, they were until that other guy showed up."

"His name is Cameron."

"You like him, and I'm scared you're going to like him more than you like me." He sounded like a small boy. One who had been abandoned. An orphan with no real purpose.

"Elliot, I might like Cameron more one day. Or if it isn't Cameron, it might be someone else. But you were the first one to show me what being in love actually felt like. You were the first one I wanted to grow old with. But that was all taken away from me." The room began to spin, but I clutched onto the sink. I closed my eyes until the dizziness passed.

"Nathan, come to the lounge. You need to sit down."

I sunk into my sofa as far as I could. My ex joined me, placing his bare feet on the coffee table.

"Why haven't you let me go, Elliot?"

"I don't think that's the question you really want to ask."

"Huh?"

"Sweetheart, there's a moment when you realize things need to change. I was on my way home to you, and then I wasn't. It was as sudden as that. And I screamed at the tangled mess inside my car as I left my body and tried my best to come to terms with the fact our lives together were over."

"And it scared the hell out of me to never see your face on the pillow next to mine every morning. Or that I'd never smell toast burning ever again," I said.

"I only burnt the toast a couple of times."

"Yes, but one of those times the flames were leaping from the toaster. Why you persisted with that antique bread burner rather than getting a pop-up model was beyond me." I thought the blue in his eyes seemed paler than usual. "But once you were gone, I missed the smell of burnt toast. Maybe that's why I agreed to work in Lucy's café?"

"Who burns toast there?" he said.

"No one, unfortunately."

"I miss Lucy. You were with her and Ben when you met me. And Ben tried to pick me up."

"And you told him there was nowhere to 'do it' at the department store, so he asked what time you finished work."

"And all that time, I was looking at you, Nathan. And you were smiling at my devilish charm."

"No. I was smiling at the man I knew I wanted to be with."

"And I smiled back."

"Ben knew he didn't have a chance."

"I know," Elliot said. "You've told me a hundred times how Lucy and Ben kept telling you to go back and ask for my number."

"And I did."

"Yes, you did." His eyes had their color back, while his complexion was as lifelike as it was when he was alive.

"Elliot, where would we be now if you had lived?"

"Still going out to dinner with Ben, Lucy, Graham, and Tony." He bit his bottom lip. "You don't see Graham and Tony anymore."

"They were your friends."

"And they became your friends as well."

I had a lump in my throat. "It felt weird seeing them after you died. I didn't want to hear the old tales you used to share with them."

"That reason doesn't even make sense, sweetheart."

"Okay, maybe I didn't want to share my grief with people who'd known you longer than me."

"They miss you, Nathan. They still talk about you and your friends from time to time. And they'd like to see your infatuation with food firsthand again."

"What? You haunt them as well?"

"No. They don't know I'm there. They've learned to live without me."

"How can I learn to live without you when you're here so often?"

"I'm only here because you want me here."

"How can I want you here? You argue with me about having sex with you. You intrude when I'm with a date."

"But you are in two minds about that American guy. And you'd love to have sex with me again."

"Oh god, yes! I'd love to take you in my arms and caress your back. I want to peel your shirt off and throw you on the carpet. I need to kiss you all over your face and your neck and your chest. And I need you to lick my earlobes and taste my lips. But the truth is, we can't anymore. You're not here, really."

"I'll make you a promise, sweetheart. I'll slip into your dreams tonight, and we'll make love one last time."

I chuckled. His blond curly locks had also returned to their original golden color, and in my mind, my fingers glided through them like I was trying on countless wedding bands.

"I love you, Elliot. I've never stopped."

"I know. To paraphrase a tedious song, the heart does like to go on and on."

"The day you died, I was at home wasting my time on social media, and the police buzzed the door. My mind was racing through a million possible reasons the cops were at our place, but losing you wasn't one of them."

"Of course. Who'd want to imagine life without me?"

"They always leave it to the female cop to break the news. At first I was in disbelief, asking what hospital you were in, but she kept repeating you weren't in a hospital. And at that moment, I *died* as well. It was never warm in this place again, and I never turned on the heater or grabbed a blanket. I just drank vodka to keep my soul from turning to ice. Well, for a week, anyway. I wasn't a good alcoholic. The hangovers were murder."

"And on the day of my funeral, your face was so red from vodka and lack of sleep that you wore sunglasses. Large garish sunglasses."

"They were Ben's. My own sunglasses were too small to cover my face."

"What were you hiding from?"

"Life without you."

He winked at me. "And here's your crossroad, my beautiful Nate. Behind door number one, you have someone who still makes you smile in faded memories, or behind door number two, you have someone who will never be me but they'll be themselves. Just as loving and caring as the person you long for behind door number one."

"Elliot, that's a decision I'm not ready to face."

"You can't keep summoning me here every time you feel fear."

"I don't believe for one second that you being here is about me not letting go. You're just as guilty of holding on."

"Then my selfishness is only hurting my one true love."

"I don't want you to go, even if you have been a nightmare to deal with."

"It's time to travel down your new path with Cameron."

"So you do remember his name!"

"Regardless, every fresh path seems frightening until we take a few first steps."

"You always do this, Elliot. You turn the blame around. You've been haunting me like it was a paying job, and now you're making out that it's been all about me not dealing with grief."

"Okay, I admit it. I found it hard to let you go, but our talk just now has made me realize something."

"What?"

"That I also have to take the first steps down my own path. The path away from you."

I lowered my head. "So this really is goodbye?"

"I guess. I mean, it has to be. I can't hang around holding you back anymore."

"I'll miss you so much. Why couldn't your hauntings be more like this?"

"Because maybe in my heart I knew if we spoke, we'd resolve things. I wasn't ready for goodbye."

His complexion faded along with the blue in his eyes. But his hair remained as rich as honeycomb. "Elliot, will I still see you in my dreams?"

"No, my love. I will haunt you no more. You have to learn to dream without me."

I puckered my lips and leaned forward, catching his tender mouth before he vanished. "Goodbye," I said. My phone rang, and I shuddered before I slapped it against my ear.

"Hello," said a voice in the background. "Hello. Are you there, Nathan?" Cameron asked on the other end. "Who was that blond guy with you at the airport?"

Chapter Seventeen

"YOU KNEW I was at the airport?" I replied.

"Not at first, Nate. It was that blond guy who made it obvious."

"He's just a friend, Cam."

"Well, it looked like he was more than a friend."

"He was, I mean, he *is* my ex."

"It looks like he's still in love with you. So, I guess that's why you've been so distant."

"Cam, it's also because our romance has been unconventional."

"Unconventional? Have you considered my circumstances? Have you considered how showing you a good time because I can is not unconventional to me?"

"Not quite, but Lucy has also mentioned that from your point of view, this is not unconventional." There was silence from his end. "Cameron, I didn't think I'd ever hear from you again."

"Would you prefer if I didn't contact you again?"

"My charming American, you can't begin to understand how happy I am to hear your voice."

"Well, Rowena put me up to it. As soon as I got home, she asked why I wasn't still in Sydney."

"How sweet. She was concerned."

"A little. But I walked in on a transvestite party, surprising her and her guests. That's why she was asking why I was home early. But when I told her why, she insisted I call you."

"That was days ago. What took you so long to call me?"

"I didn't want to at first, but Roger, or Rowena on any given day, kept badgering me. So here I am, calling you."

"Cam, I'm sorry I made you feel less than a boyfriend. The reason was that blond."

"Your ex?"

"My ex. I didn't realize how much of a hold he had on me. Can you forgive me?"

"It all depends."

"On what?"

"I have to go. Check your email in ten minutes, then give me an answer." He made a kissy sound over the phone, then hung up. Ten minutes later, I checked my email. As soon as I saw what he sent, I emailed him back. He rang straight away.

"It's only one time zone different to yours in Sydney," he replied. "So, you have no reason to feel jetlagged."

"But you'll be jetlagged."

"Nate, I wasn't too bad when I visited you in Sydney."

"That's because I met you in your hotel at night. Between lovemaking, I napped, while you looked tired when you came to my place."

"Well, if you hadn't yelled at me, I could have taken a nap. Adrenaline and a broken heart kept me awake."

"Cam, it wasn't you who I yelled at, and I'll explain when we see each other in a few days."

"I'm glad Roger talked me into calling you."

There was a momentary pause. "He, and she, is a wise butler and maid. Oh, one last thing."

"What?"

"I love you."

"Wow, you've floored me. I love you too, my outspoken Australian." He made another kissy sound. "See you in Tokyo, my love."

"Definitely! I'll greet you at the door of our hotel in a kimono with a cup of sake."

"As long as you don't put on a wig. One transvestite is enough for me, thank you."

"Thank you for choosing somewhere I won't be jetlagged, Cam."

"I also picked it because they still have a Tower Records store somewhere."

"Oh, okay," I replied, not really knowing what he meant. "See you, my love."

"Bye, beautiful."

"Can't wait to see you, gorgeous."

"Me too, darling. Bye."

"Bye."

It was official. We now sounded like one of those newlyweds that you cringe at when you're within earshot. My eyes darted around the room for a sign of Elliot, and I was half-disappointed when I realized he was gone for good. But I needed to do something else before my rendezvous in Japan. I called to see what Lucy and Ben were doing the next day.

"THANKS FOR MEETING me here," I said. I popped the cork on the bottle of champagne I'd brought. Lucy and Ben held their glasses as I poured.

"Nathan, I know I'm not overly sentimental, but I'm glad you're doing this," said Ben.

"It's something I needed to do."

"But it's something I need to do as well."

"Me too," said Lucy. "And I can't believe we hadn't done it sooner."

We raised our glasses above Elliot's headstone. One woman in a black skirt and top watched our toast to my lost love. While her outfit was somber, her face was kind as she nodded in approval at our antics.

A breeze blew as we sipped to a man who was taken from our world too soon, and in that gust, I heard Elliot whisper, "Farewell." Ben handed me a hanky, but it was Lucy who took it and dabbed my cheeks.

"I never said this to you, Nathan, but I was a bit jealous of your relationship," she confessed.

"Yeah," said Ben. "It made me smile when you'd finish each other's sentences, yet neither of you knew you were doing it. You were the perfect couple."

I grinned.

Lucy pointed down a pathway. "Speaking of couples, look who's coming our way."

"You invited them, didn't you, Nathan?" Ben asked. I nodded. "And they brought more champagne."

I hugged Tony as Lucy embraced Graham like a relative who'd just returned safely from war. Then Tony clutched onto Ben as my friend quietly sobbed. "Don't cry, Ben," he said. "Or I'll start."

"It's been too long," I said as I held Graham.

I took two more glasses from my backpack and handed them to the couple. Ben poured.

"I'd like to propose a toast to someone who brought us all together," I said. I raised my glass, and the others followed. "It was Ben who tried to pick you up, Elliot, but it was me who shared your life, briefly. But in that time, I knew there'd be no one else who was as sassy as you. No offense, Ben."

"None taken," he replied.

"And I knew no one would make me feel the way you made me feel. But that's the thing, isn't it? There's no one who makes me feel the way Lucy or Ben do, either. And you introduced us to Graham and Tony, because you wanted to share the way they made *you* feel. And I know Lucy and Ben made you feel special, because you were and still are special to me. That's a feeling that will never be replaced. We all have our own way of sharing our own special magic with others. And I'm honored I was chosen as one of the people you shared the magic that is you, Elliot."

"And thank you, Nathan, for sharing yourself with me," whispered the breeze.

"I heard that," said Ben.

"Me too," said Graham.

"Me three," said Lucy.

"I'm trying to pretend I didn't hear it," Tony added.

Lucy put her arm around my shoulders. "It sounds like Elliot approves of your speech."

"It takes a lot to let go," I replied.

"But you're taking the first step."

Chapter Eighteen

VIDEO SCREENS BURST with bubblegum colors, demanding attention high in the skyscrapers above. Taxi drivers watched vigilantly for potential fares. Fashionable crowds filled the sidewalk, some darting about in order to meet friends on time. And a mishmash of large and small eateries flaunted plastic replicas of their menus in their front windows.

"I love Tokyo," I said.

"We just got here," Cameron replied.

"But you've got to admit, it's pretty cool!"

My charming man nodded. "It's manga on steroids!"

I kissed him. Some of the younger passersby grinned in approval.

"Any idea where this restaurant is?" I asked.

"I have the address in Japanese on my phone. I'll show it to the taxi driver."

Several old box-shaped cars painted in pastel hues waited at the traffic lights. We hailed one, and his back door opened automatically, like magic. Cam showed our driver his phone, and soon we were zipping around this metropolis.

We arrived at an upmarket sushi bar, and after stepping down some stairs, a polite woman greeted us. Five other patrons sat around the chef's preparation area, so we quickly joined them where our own bottle of sake was waiting. We opted for the 'you gauge what you think we'd like' option, allowing the experienced chef to second-guess our tastes.

I was in heaven with every bite, as each small work of culinary artistry melted with the perfect balance of flavors in my mouth. Traces of ginger, sesame, and wasabi greeted my tongue, knowing when to make their initial welcome and when to come back for further titillation.

"You're really enjoying that sushi, Nate."

"Yum! I've never eaten sushi this good."

Cameron refilled our sake cups, and we drank while holding hands under our corner of the table. I missed my mouth once, spilling a little alcohol on my shirt. My man giggled like a boy playing a prank on a schoolmate. I felt sheepish as the chef offered me a cloth and the other patrons smiled in amusement.

Eventually we ambled out of the restaurant with directions to some local gay bars and, after a short taxi ride, got out in front of a door where a drag queen in oversized glasses waved us in. Vodka and orange juice added to our gaiety, and soon we were barhopping, meeting local bears and their Western admirers, singing karaoke in front of bewildered onlookers, and dancing the night away with a younger crowd.

We couldn't remember the name of our hotel at first, but eventually the patient driver made sense of what we were trying to say.

We threw off our clothes and squeezed into the shower the moment we opened our door. My charming man stood under the stream of water, his dark wet hair falling over his forehead. I parted it, giving tiny kisses from his hairline to the tip of his nose. He grabbed me and planted his lips against mine. Droplets trickled in all directions, working their way down our bodies, cooling us from our own heat.

I TRIED TO peer at Cam through one eye, but the sunlight blinded me. Like a thrashing whale in fear of its fate, I stumbled around our hotel room until I made it to the curtains, almost ripping them from their rails as I pulled them shut. I fell onto my hands and knees and crawled toward our bed.

"Hungover?"

"Yeah," I grunted.

"There's iced coffee in our fridge."

"There is?"

"Remember? You insisted on picking some up on our way home."

"I did?"

"Yes, you did."

"Hold on."

"Hold on what?"

"I'm about to be sick."

"THIS IS STRONG coffee," said Cameron.

"It's good coffee," I replied.

"You don't find this strong?"

"It's better than most I had in Europe."

Two hours later, we sat in bed, naked, clutching our beverages.

"That was the best night I've ever had with you, Nate."

"Same," I smirked.

"So was that our first successful date?"

"We had fun in New York. And we grew close in Sydney."

"No, Nathan. In New York, I was a plastic fool."

"A plastic fool?"

"You know what I mean. I was showing off. God, I even sang to you. What an idiot!"

I held his hand. "My charming man, that was one of the most romantic things anyone has ever done for me."

"But I didn't know you well enough to take that chance."

"I liked it. Your Aunt Beverley liked it."

"Yeah, you both liked it. But you didn't *love* it."

"Okay, at the time, I was a bit taken aback, but Cam, it's going to be one of those moments I'll look back on and treasure as our relationship grows."

He beamed as he looked out the window. "I have to ask you something, Nathan."

"Yes?"

"Tell me about that blond."

"Oh, him. He's brash, outspoken, and hilarious. And he's caring, loving, and one of the most empathic people I knew."

"You knew? Don't you mean you 'know'?"

"It's my way of letting him go."

Cam gazed at me. "He sounds like a ghost. He sounds like he's shaped you in some way, and you haven't let go."

"No, no, no, Cameron. Trust me. I've let go. You have nothing to fear from Elliot. From here on in, you are my partner, my lover, my boyfriend."

"I'm not so sure."

"I thought after last night, you'd know I was yours."

He lay back. "Tell me more about you and Elliot."

"Look, it's true, he was the reason I was distant in New York."

"I was distant, too."

"But I could have had fun from all your kindness. We went to some great places, and while I'm still paying off my European trip, I got to see New York."

"And Tokyo."

"And Tokyo. Look, Elliot was perfect for me at a certain time of my life. But that time is over, and our future as a long-term couple was never meant to be. And in front of me, I have a guy called Cameron. He's not Elliot. He could never be if he tried. And I don't want him to be. I want to hear more of his crazy serenades. Let him show me more of his New York. Let me show him more of my Sydney. And continue making love in whatever part of the world we find ourselves in."

He gasped, then sat up. "You know, I really thought that Tokyo would be our last stop. Rowena was right about you. It's amazing what wisdom she has when she's drunk on gin."

"It's sad that that wisdom doesn't extend to her fashion sense."

"You're wicked, Mr. Jones."

"I've heard you say some catty things too, Mr. Charlton."

We kissed briefly.

"So, Nate, how are we going to work this long-distance affair?"

"Don't call it an affair. It sounds too sordid."

"Sorry, but you do see our problem."

"What about six months at your place, then six months at mine? Spring and summer in each city."

"Sounds romantic. I can just hear what my dad will say when I tell him I'm not ready to find a career because half my time I'll live in Australia."

"Hey, you could open an online store or something. We could work it together. It won't matter where we live. But for the time being, let's enjoy our honeymoon."

"Our honeymoon? Yeah, why not? It's our first adventure that's foreign to us both. What a great way to start a real relationship."

"Let's take on this town. I need breakfast."

"I think it's lunchtime."

"I need lunch!"

I reached for his head and messed up his hair. He jumped out of bed, grabbed my ankles, and slid me down the mattress. As I tried to sit up, he pounced on me, meeting me face to face.

And in his eyes, I saw myself. A young man looking for love and shaking off the reasons that previously had held him back.

And in his lips, I saw the endless pleasure we would share. The kisses that would say what we felt when words could no longer.

And in his face, I saw the man who would teach me to love without fear of loss. The man I was willing to grow with in new directions. And it didn't matter if those directions had skyscrapers, harbors, a Taj Mahal, or an Eiffel Tower. For this was an adventure that was just beginning.

NATE'S LAST TANGO

Chapter One

"I'M NERVOUS," I said. But my boyfriend, Cam, didn't hear me. Fortunately, his butler, Roger, did.

"Here you go, Nate." The loyal servant placed a garishly green cocktail in my hand, complete with a little umbrella. "This will make you so chilled, the next few hours will feel like a hippie folk festival."

If only that were the truth. I was about to meet Cameron's parents for the first time, and both he and Roger were busy preparing canapés. They insisted I was as much of a guest as the others were, so I wasn't to help with the catering.

Instead, I gazed out the window of my boyfriend's swish New York apartment, trying to imagine what a middle-aged couple who had made their fortune in the funeral trade would be like. My first thought was something as creepy as an older Gomez and Morticia from *The Addams Family*.

And with that vision came a list of odd relatives I hadn't met yet. Perhaps a short hunchback that rang church bells. An older brother who slept in the basement during the day and showed off his unusually sharp fangs to unsuspecting women at night. Or a haggard stepsister who kidnapped the neighborhood pets and offered them to pagan gods during midnight rituals.

I watched my boyfriend. He was trying to make art out of smoked salmon and flatbread, but somehow he kept adding too much mayo. The result was something that looked like a squeezed pimple rather than anything you'd put in your mouth. As always, Roger was at his side to fix his creations, and as a pair they worked well.

Through his chic designer glasses, Cam scrutinized what Rog was trying to show him, and he understood until his butler tucked, folded, or did whatever was necessary to make my boyfriend's attempts look presentable. Although my man wasn't perfect, that was the very reason I loved him. He'd try. And he had enough people around to support him. His parents had to be equally as supportive, surely.

Any moment they'd swan in the front door, having just flown in from Paris, where they had stayed the night because they'd decided to eat dinner in that romantic city on a whim. His mum, or mom as these Americans say, would offer me her hand adorned in a teal glove and wait for me to kiss it.

His dad would check me out, and while he shook my hand all businesslike, it wouldn't be until later that his real nature would come out. He'd pull out a joint and tell us about his wild days; of wearing a leather jacket, having wall-to-wall lovers, and the heavy rock band he fronted with regular top-ten hits.

"Would you like another cocktail, Nate?" Roger asked.

"No, I've hardly—" My glass was empty.

"Your mind is preoccupied. Let me get you another."

"No. I don't want to be drunk before they arrive."

"Have a cocktail," said Cam as he ran his finger under a tap after burning it on poached chicken. "If I was in your shoes, I'd be nervous as well."

Roger took the glass out of my hand and promptly made me another green drink. With the first sip, my mind wandered even more, back to last month.

CAM AND I were in Barcelona. We were walking through a crazy unfinished church whose spires were so high, peeping toms could hide in their countless platforms and spy on this city of love. I kissed my man in what seemed to be an alien octopus's lair. White arms reached down from the roof with glass eyes attached to their joints. White pop-art flowers littered the roof, while Jesus swung from a jellyfish just above the altar.

"My mind thinks it's on acid, but my body knows better," said Cam.

"Imagine if Sydney's Opera House was built around Gaudi's time," I pondered.

"There'd be a dragon's mouth as a stage in the main concert hall, and the seats would be tiered on its tail."

"No. That sounds too normal."

"Okay then, what would the Opera House be like if Picasso designed it?"

"Picasso wasn't an architect."

"Work with me, Nate."

"No one would be able to sit on the seats. They'd be jagged and uncomfortable."

"And what if Tom of Finland drew the initial sketches?"

"There'd be pillars in the shape of—" I chuckled.

"And the stage would look like a giant open, you know, after—"

"Not a place for high art." I grinned.

He nodded and took my hand.

"WHERE ARE YOU, Nate?" my boyfriend asked. He was now heating sugar to make caramel.

"Back on our trip."

"Were you at that street party?"

"No. I was at Gaudí's church."

He smiled as he kept carefully stirring the pot of toffee. Meanwhile, my thoughts wandered back to Barcelona.

THERE WERE SO many narrow side streets that had to be discovered. So we strolled, losing ourselves in the clothes and assorted gifts that beckoned us from the shop windows.

"What do you think of this one, Nate?" Cameron held what looked like a mini lime-colored school bag.

"It will be hard to match with an outfit."

"Maybe I'm going through a new phase."

"What phase is that? Ultra-camp?"

"Very funny, my sarcastic Australian. No, I meant I'm discovering color."

"That's not color. That's someone's idea of a joke."

"What about this one?" He pointed to a red bag.

"That would work better in New York."

"Nathan, the green one would also work in New York."

The tall shop assistant finally butted in. "Can I help you with anything, gentlemen?"

"Just looking," I replied.

"May I suggest"—he took a cardboard box from behind the counter and opened it—"this one!"

It was still a miniature school bag but one that demanded respect. Its distressed black leather and oversized tarnished zipper had us drooling like men in a sex club.

"Oh yes!" I said. "This is the one, Cam."

"I've gone to bag heaven," he replied. "We'll take it!"

As the assistant was tapping on the computerized cash register, my boyfriend was stroking his purchase like a pet that needed calming. Soon we were out of the store, our feet taking us in the direction of several hipster cafés. When we agreed on which had the best-looking waiter, we took our seats.

"I'm in love," said Cam.

"I know," I replied.

"With my bag."

"I know. I owe that shop assistant a heap of gratitude. Trust me, Cam, if you bought that green one, it would have sat in the wardrobe forever wondering why it had been banished."

"I'm glad we're doing Barcelona."

"Because of the shopping?"

"No, Nate, because of us. Yeah, we had Tokyo and it was fun. Two scallywags on vacation."

"Scallywags? Since when did you become an upper-class British pirate?"

"Roger referred to us as scallywags before we left for the airport. It's a word."

"Lime-green bags and scallywags? Bring back my boyfriend!"

The waiter arrived to take our orders. I asked for a bottle of wine before we checked the menu. He was quick with a recommendation, then left us to peruse.

"We got the sexy one to serve us," I stated. "And see how calm he is?"

"Nate, we're not having this debate again, are we?"

"Not a debate, just an observation."

"I get it. He's not underpaid like American waiters. You've said it over and over again."

"It's criminal. Imagine if I worked as a waiter in your home country—"

"Nate, it's your home country as well at the moment."

"I'd never make a decent wage. I'd never have backpacked with my friends to Europe. I'd never have met you in Prague."

"I know, Nathan, I know. Now, can we drop this subject once and for all?"

Our waiter returned with our wine and promptly filled our glasses. We apologized for not looking at the menu yet, so he quickly ran through some of the specials. We ordered from his suggestions, then toasted each other after he left.

"Before your rant about American wages and scallywags, I was talking about how nice it is to be in Spain with you." He held his glass close to his cheek. "We've still got half a week left, but if there's something I've learned about myself, it is how much in love I am with you, Nathan."

"I know."

"Do you? Do you know how I feel when I wake up and the first thing I see is your face either sleeping or staring back at me?"

"That's creepy. Do I really stare?"

"Nate, I'm being romantic. Shut up for a minute."

I kept quiet. We both held our wine glasses, yet neither of us sipped. He spoke about his own cautious beginning to our relationship and how he's learned that love is not a fairy tale. I was going to interrupt, saying that our relationship *was* like a fairy tale as no one else I knew traveled as much as us, but I stopped myself.

"What I like most about you," he said, "is that you make me laugh. Sure, Roger makes me laugh, but you have a dark sense of humor, and it's rubbing off on me."

"Friends can make you laugh."

"But I don't gaze at them after they've made me laugh and think how lucky I am that this person is in love with me."

"EARTH CALLING NATE," Roger called. "Your daydreams are traveling faster than the speed of light. What's on your mind?"

"How lucky I am," I replied.

Cam gazed at me as our grins widened.

"Another drink?" Roger asked.

"Of course. There's a lot to celebrate."

Again I stared at the Manhattan skyline as my favorite butler worked his magic with the cocktail shaker. But New York was not where my mind was at.

THE EUROPEAN CITY breathed us in, making us part of its after-hours sophistication. Our shoes clicked like a flamenco dancer's fingers as we stepped on the paved streets. The latest fashion called us to the overlit windows of the many chic outlets. Shirts with angular collars and trousers of light blue had me dressing, and undressing, my charming American in my mind. The need to shop had not subsided.

"You'd look good in that, Nate," he said.

"I was picturing *you* in that outfit," I replied.

"I think I'm more..." Cam pointed to a classic tan jacket.

"It would match your eyes, but I think it's something I would wear rather than you."

"Remember how I borrowed that suit jacket of yours for Sally's dinner party?"

"Yeah. Strange choice, but it looked good on you."

"Our fashion sense is melding. Soon we'll look the same, Nate."

"How long have you liked that suit jacket?"

"I admit, when I first saw you in it, I thought nah! But after one of our theatre jaunts, we sat at Kev's Deli, and you were wearing it. I couldn't take my eyes off my stylish Australian."

"Do you mean you couldn't take your eyes off your stylish Australian, or your stylish Australian's jacket?"

"Both. I thought to myself, *my man has taste*."

I held his hand as we continued to stroll. Nineteenth-century streetlamps lit the bright yellow walls on a small street we ventured down. A golden glow was cast. A few random stragglers smiled at us as they made their way past.

"Why did you talk me out of visiting Paris?" Cameron asked.

"Look at this place. It's magic."

"Yes, but Paris is the city of love."

"But Barcelona is Paris lite, with people willing to share their city."

"What are you saying? Paris people aren't nice?"

"They're nice, but this is a smaller city, so of course it's friendlier. And just wait until you see the gay scene tomorrow night."

"Paris has a gay scene."

"Paris has a gay scene like New York or Sydney have a gay scene. Disjointed. The gays still party here instead of picking up someone on an app." He gave me a quizzical look. "I'll prove it to you tomorrow night. Lucy, Ben, and I had a blast. I'll just have to make sure our hotel room is equipped with hangover cures."

We approached a street where a multitude of umbrellas in every color greeted us from above. They had been strung up from windowsills and each housed a light, turning them into lanterns. But people were crowded at the far end, watching something around the corner. Then we heard it.

"You're right, Nathan Jones. This place is magical."

We hustled over in their direction and saw the purple haze of the night sky come to life with firecrackers. The street folk reveled as they held the magic sticks that spewed sparks high above their heads. A band played while older women danced as if long-lost passions had been rediscovered.

"I need to learn to be as spontaneous as these Spaniards," I said.

"You're better than you were, Nate."

I looked at Cam. His face flickered in the bouncing light, while flames leaped, reflecting in his glasses. He noticed me gazing. His nose rubbed against mine before our lips locked in a kiss that lingered. Men cheered, children laughed, and then, people clapped.

And all this time, I was an addict to his kiss. A spell so potent the world didn't exist. His tongue slipped in, caressing me, making me light-headed. As his head tilted, I fell deeper, trying to become one with my Cameron. His man scent was the drug that again had me hooked.

He broke away, grabbed the back of my head, and brought his lips to my forehead. This moist touch spirited my worries away while the bristly stubble made me want to lick and play with every part of him that reminded me he was a man. The tip of his nose once again led a trail down mine before my cheeky bugger dabbed me with the point of his tongue—a paintbrush stroke to the end of my nose.

I chuckled, but as I was about to wipe my lover's mark, his mischievous tongue entered my mouth, calling my own tongue to action. With our bodies on automatic pilot, we explored what passion could be.

A warmth that goes beyond lust, yet lust was very much part of the journey. Tenderness lay with it. Fondness whispered in my ear, reminding me I'm in a safe place.

This was the perfect moment. We both knew it, and we didn't need to say it. Finally, after our initial rocky start, we were in synch. We were connected. We were in love.

"Let's go back to our hotel room," Cam purred.

"I had the same thought," I replied.

We ran like outlaws being chased, sprinting past puzzled locals. We rushed into the elevator. Lips locked all the way up.

With his hand pressed to my chest, he walked me backward toward the bed. I fell willingly, bouncing lightly on the mattress. He stood above me like a demigod about to send me to a magic kingdom of brazen nymphs, playful centaurs, and wicked cherubs. And I'd go wherever he led.

One by one, he popped his buttons before flinging his shirt, discarding it like yesterday's news. I sat up and tugged at his belt buckle. His jeans slithered to his feet as a welcome friend extended a greeting under his crisp white jocks. My hand caressed the cotton.

Cam reached for my shirt, but I waved him away. With one jerk, his underwear fell, and I pulled him by his finest feature onto the bed. Wet trails were marking my jeans as his knob rubbed against the denim. My arms wrapped his naked body; my man slightly vulnerable yet secure in my embrace.

We kissed again as he groaned for skin on skin.

"YOUR MIND REALLY is on another planet, isn't it, Nate?" Cameron asked as he tasted toffee from a wooden spoon. "You can't hide anything from me, Mr. Jones."

"You're blushing," Roger stated. "It's not hard to work out what part of your trip you're reminiscing about."

"Yeah, caught red-handed," I confessed. "My memories were X-rated."

Cam shared a grin as wicked as a cat who'd dined on the family goldfish. "You're thinking about that time you stayed dressed in our hotel room, aren't you, Nate?"

"That doesn't sound sexual," said Roger.

"Believe me, it was sexual. I eventually got his clothes off."

Roger comically rolled his eyes. "Another drink, Nate?"

"I've still got—" I looked at my glass. "Geez, I'm going through these like—"

"Zsa Zsa Gabor went through husbands?"

"Who?"

"Never mind, dearie. I'll get you another drink."

As Rog made his way back to the kitchen, I felt a strange shiver. Like a ghost walked through me. And with the serenity of my loving man pouring caramel over a homemade ice-cream cake and his butler meticulously measuring the alcohol for my cocktail, came an unwelcome sense of dread.

"YOU AUSTRALIANS HAVE such a quaint accent," said Cam's mom. "It's kind of British, but it's kind of not."

"Don't patronize the young boy, dear," her husband reprimanded.

"I'm not. I'm not patronizing you, am I, Nathan?"

I shook my head.

"See? I know the type of man my Cameron would pick." She studied my face. "You're an earth sign, aren't you?"

"I'm a what?" I asked.

"An earth sign. Let me guess. A Taurean."

"I'm a Virgo."

"A Virgo. You can't be. Not with those ears."

"Another drink, Mrs. Charlton?" Roger asked. He'd already slipped another cocktail in my hand.

"Yes, dear. Can I have a martini?"

"Right away, madam."

So there we were, seated on the modular lounge. Mr. Charlton sat on the edge of the bit that juts out, with a scotch on the rocks in one hand and his smartphone in the other. He kept checking the electronic device as if it beckoned him through mental telepathy.

But what I couldn't take my eyes off was his comb-over. It was as if somebody had drawn straight lines across his scalp with a permanent marker. Surely, with his money, he could have visited a hair replacement clinic.

Mrs. Charlton was charming. Ditzy, but charming. She finally got my name right after five attempts, mistaking me for Mark, Maverick, Norbert, and Niles, in that order. She had a habit of smoking indoors, saying she didn't respect all these new rules and regulations. And she had Cam's smile. Cam's mesmerizing smile that made me feel at home in her presence.

"You're leaving Cameron?" she asked me.

"Only for a month," I replied.

"What have you done to this poor boy?" she asked her son.

"What do you mean?" he replied.

"Oh, there's no marital problems if that's what you think," I said.

"Well, there must be some reason such a gorgeous man like you is leaving my son for such a long time after... How long has it been?"

"Six months," Cam replied.

"Six months of freeloading in our son's apartment," said the father. His eyes were glued to his phone.

"Dad. Dad, look at me when I'm talking to you. You know Nate and I have gone into business."

"You call that a business?"

"Designer T-shirts *are* a business."

"And we're making good money," I said. "We're making several hundred a month after paying the local artists, but we're going to expand to online after I make my trip back to Sydney."

"You see, you're going back to Sydney," Mrs. Charlton interrupted. "Why, Cameron? What have you done to this poor boy that he has to leave you so soon?"

"My friend, Lucy, is interested in opening a Sydney version of our store. She currently runs a coffee shop, but with her expertise, the new Art-Wear Shop should be up and running by the time I return to New York."

"The Art-Wear Shop down under. How sweet. Isn't that sweet, Carl? And a trustworthy Virgo is going down there to make sure our son's business is a success."

"It's not just *my* business," Cam said, correcting his mother.

"Shouldn't you set up the online store first?" Cam's dad asked. "Before large Sydney rents add to your ongoing budget!"

"Now, Carl. You used to be so kind and supportive to Cameron when he was growing up. You listened to his dreams and encouraged him. You wiped his tears when he was fearful. What happened to the man I married?"

"What happened is that we all got older and wiser, some more than others." He looked back to his phone. "And in my own way, I am being supportive. I'm just saying that the next logical step is an online store. Their current local shop only makes a few hundred a month, which is nowhere near enough to cover commercial rent in Manhattan. And now they're thinking Sydney? Yeah, go boys! A second version of a store that is already losing money."

And so the parents went on. At some stage, Roger oversupplied Cam and me with cocktails, as both of us realized we had a drink in each hand. I downed one and drank half the other. As the parents droned on, we were saved by Roger's alter ego.

His continuity error to the evening was disruptively noticeable, yet it was a godsend. The butler was now Rowena in a backless cocktail dress, appropriately black in color, and a dark wig that could rival Marge Simpson's in height. She wheeled in a stylish drinks trolley and continued mixing more concoctions than we could drink in one night.

"Tell me, Nathan," Cam's mom said in an obvious effort to change the subject. "Tell me about your past loves."

I looked to my boyfriend.

"Don't worry," he said. "She always asks everyone she meets."

"Yes, I do. You can learn so much about where a person has been and where they are headed to."

I looked to Cam again for a way out, but he smiled and gave me an approving nod.

"I've had a few that are hardly worth mentioning."

"But they wrote the story of Nathan. A Virgo's story."

"Go on, Nate," my boyfriend said. "Tell my mom about Elliot."

"Are you sure?" I asked.

"I don't think my wife is sure about anything." The father was still glued to his phone.

"Nathan, tell me about Elliot," his mother bade.

"Well, Elliot was different to Cameron. Queenier, if you like. And he had a heart as big as the world. But he knew how to cut through the bullshit. You see, he could console you when you were down, but if you were ready to give up, he'd slap it out of you with his words. That's why we all loved him. That's why the sun shone through the clouds just for him. Or why the world would grin back as he smiled. Why that blond curl in the middle of his forehead—"

"Oops!" Rowena spilled scotch on Carl's skull. Strands of hair were now covering his face like dangling spider legs. It was the most expressionless he looked all night.

"Oh dear," was all Cam's mother said.

Like a trooper, our cocktail-dress-wearing butler used his sleeve to wipe Carl dry. Yet Mr. Charlton continued sitting perfectly still, even as the strands found new paths across his face.

"Is something burning?" my boyfriend asked.

"I can't smell a thing," I reported.

"The couch is singed," Rowena replied.

"Oh, sorry. It must have come from my cigarette ash!" Cam's mom proclaimed.

"What are you talking about?" the father grumbled. "My wife is clumsy but she—"

Our hired help picked up the soda siphon and aimed it at the scorched material. She somehow slipped, missing her target.

Cam and his mom were drenched. Droplets dripped from the bottom of Mrs. Charlton's dangly earrings, and Cam couldn't see a thing as the water covered his glasses like spray paint. He stood, untucked his shirt, and wiped them, only smearing the droplets over the lenses.

Mr. Charlton grunted like a moody ape while Mrs. Charlton chuckled like a hyena. I started giggling too, somehow from the floor. *Why am I stretched out on the carpet?* Cam saw the joke and slowly worked himself into a full belly laugh. As his laughter subsided, he looked to Rowena who simply sighed in relief.

Chapter Two

"YOU LOOK LIKE death warmed up," said Lucy.

"And you flew business class," Ben added.

"Yeah, with a stopover in Vancouver and nearly a day in the air," I replied.

This was my greeting at Sydney International Airport. My two best friends unsympathetic to my out-of-whack body clock, helping me pick out my luggage from the conveyor belt.

"So is it still lurve?" Lucy asked. "That grin says it all, Nathan."

"Are your in-laws the rich dream parents you were hoping for?" Ben asked. "Oh. I see. Is that a reaction face, or are you feeling some diarrhea coming on?"

"Trust me, diarrhea is preferable to spending an evening with them again."

"What did they do?"

"It's not so much what they did; it's how Cam's dad talks to the family, and me for that matter. He's attitude on overload." I reached forward to grab my suitcase, but Ben beat me to it.

"Is that it?" he asked.

"That's it," I replied.

"Only one bag?"

"Only one bag."

"Where're all your designer New York outfits? Where's the dozens of Art-Wear T-shirts for the Sydney store? Where're all the gifts you've bought me and Lucy?"

"Come now, Ben," said Lucy. "You know Nate probably made a list itemizing everything he had to pack a week before he booked his flight. Then revised it every day without fail."

"Why did I ever ask you two to pick me up from the airport?"

"You felt sorry for us peasants," Ben replied, pretending to struggle with my bag. I stepped ahead, prompting us to walk toward the parking lot.

"It's still Cameron's money, not mine."

My friends shared a droll look.

"Hey, we've set up a business. That's how I make *my* money."

"And I bet you budget by eating at cheap franchise burger joints," said Lucy.

"And you shop at secondhand stores for last year's designer fashion," Ben added.

"And when you're really skint, you and Cam busk duets for the evening commuters."

"That can't be right. Have you heard Nate sing? They'd pay him to shut up."

"Yeah, yeah, yeah," I replied. "You may not believe me, but I do watch what I spend."

"Of course you do," Ben said. He stopped in his tracks and put on his best upper-class accent. "'Oh, Cameron. Have you seen this thing on the menu? Noodles. Like spaghetti but Asian. What a novel idea. We must tell Cook.'"

Lucy and I chuckled. "Admit it," she said. "Life isn't tough for our Nathan." We continued walking.

"I have a comfortable life," I replied. "But I contribute any way I can."

"Yeah, like in the bedroom," said Ben. "You've found what I want, a sugar daddy my own age."

"That's a bit tough," said Lucy. "Love knows no bank balance."

"Sorry, Nate. I didn't mean to be offensive."

"Trust me. I wasn't offended. The day we stop talking to each other like this is the day we stop being friends. And Ben, a *sugar daddy* can't technically be your own age."

He nodded, feebly.

We had arrived at Lucy's sporty Corolla. She popped the boot, and Ben placed my suitcase inside.

"Where are you going?" I asked Ben as he gave me a kiss on the cheek.

"I have a man to see."

"I offered to drop him off, but he insisted on driving his car," Lucy explained.

"To the airport?" I questioned. "You paid for parking at the airport when you didn't need to? It seems I'm not the only one living in the lap of luxury."

"I have a hot stud waiting for me," said Ben. "And sex knows no budget." He waved frenetically as he skipped toward the elevator.

"What's he on?" I asked.

"Get in. I'll tell you in the car." I did as she said. She carefully reversed, and soon we were inching our way out of the airport, bumper to bumper. "Ben's got a new bonk buddy."

"Don't you mean f—"

"I'm being polite. His name is Fox, and this is their third get-together."

"His name is Fox?"

"He's quite nice."

"His name is Fox?"

"He's not bad looking."

"His name is Fox?"

"I had the same reaction when Ben told me. But, like I said, it's their third get-together, so…" She shrugged.

"Three times is usually when Ben loses interest."

"Even if he's not really into the guy. Remember that one we called Shakespeare?"

"Yeah," I replied. "He couldn't string two words together when we tried to speak to him. Did you ever tell Ben we called him Shakespeare?"

"Of course I did. Ben thought it was hilarious. Besides, Ben comes up with tragic names for *my* love interests."

"Have you and Ben got a name for Cam?"

There was no reply.

"Hmm. So what do you call my boyfriend?"

"We started with Richie Rich, but that was too naff."

"Go on."

"The only others were Nate's Lottery Win and the Man with the Golden Gun."

"Huh?"

"It was my bad attempt at sexual innuendo, and Ben didn't get it either. And then he was just Cam once we realized you weren't coming back to Sydney."

"I'm here now."

"For a visit."

"But I'm here."

"Yes, and we haven't seen you for six months. It's not like you can't afford to see us more often."

"We've spoken on social media."

"It's not the same as having you here, Nathan."

Lucy's Corolla finally made it to the main road, and we were on our way to her place. I was going to pay for a hotel room, but she insisted I stay on her couch. Considering I was missing her and Ben, it was an offer too good to refuse.

"So what's been happening in your love life?" I asked.

She chuckled.

"That bad, huh?"

"I think I'm re-virginating. I know it's a cliché, but all the best ones are either married or gay."

"Have you been dating?"

She smiled to herself. "Yeah. I've met some nice guys, three in fact, and I had a good time. But nothing eventuated. Nate, my darling, count your lucky stars you found Cameron."

"If you remember rightly, Cam found me."

"And boy, you were hesitant. Prince Charming falls in your lap and we still had to drag you kicking and screaming into romance."

"You're right, and I thank you for that. He's my slightly eccentric, charming American."

"You *have* fallen."

I paused. "I shouldn't boast. Sorry, Lucy."

"No, go on. I'm happy for you, Nate." My phone notified me of a text message. "Was that Artoo-Detoo I just heard from the backseat?"

"It's corny, I know."

"Kind of geeky, but not corny. Are you going to get that, Nate?"

"My bag is out of reach unless I take my seat belt off. We're near your place. It can wait." I turned to look at my hand luggage just to confirm I couldn't reach it. Then I decided I didn't want to be a slave to my demanding communication device. "What were we saying before we got interrupted?"

"I can tell you want to answer it."

"Lucy, I'm with you at the moment."

"But unless you've popped in an Australian sim card, it can only be a message from lover boy. A love memo on your mobile phone, or do you call it a cell phone now that you're all Manhattan-like?"

"Stop teasing. It will wait. Weren't we talking about *your* love life?"

"No, we were talking about yours, Nate. I've often wondered when you finally realized you were in love with Cam."

"In Tokyo, which I call our unofficial honeymoon. But watching him in his seat while we were on the plane back to Sydney, well, I just knew. It was more than his looks. It was the way we both grew to know each other before that, and we both sensed we were content. As if the connection we first had when we met was now solid. It had mileage."

"Mileage? Not kilometers?"

"I'm babbling, aren't I?"

"Nate, love makes everyone babble. It's nice to know you are in love."

We pulled into the driveway of an older block of flats in the stylish inner-western suburb of Dulwich Hill. While I was gone, Lucy had sold her soul to the devil in order to find the deposit to enter Sydney's overpriced real estate market.

"I like this place," I said. "It has character."

"These older places have more room inside than the new ones. Nathan! You're eyeing your hand luggage."

"I'm not."

"Then what did I just say?"

"It has a good floor plan."

She rolled her eyes. "Close enough."

I did, however, dive into the backseat once I was out of the car to fish out my phone. Yes, the message was from Cam. The corners of my mouth must have reached my ears as I swiped the screen to read his memorandum of love.

"What's the matter, Nathan?" Lucy asked.

I stared at the words, wondering if there was a typo. But it was hard to misinterpret the text. My friend, her Corolla, and the concrete below my feet didn't exist. The screen of the phone filled my vision like CinemaScope.

I tried to speak, but my voice was caught on a hook in my throat. I was in a world devoid of common sense. *How could this be?* There were no answers. After all, I wasn't even sure of the questions.

Chapter Three

AT ELEVEN AT night, I texted. By then, it was eight in the morning in New York and I had already spent the afternoon pacing, crying, screaming, and talking Lucy's ear off, trying to find a reason.

Cam returned my text, so Lucy shuffled me off into her room with her laptop and closed the door behind me. I clicked on the Skype icon.

"I deserve an explanation." I got straight to the point.

"I just need some time alone," he replied. He sat on the lounge in pajamas while the sun peeked through the clouds outside his large windows.

"How much time? A month? A year? Give me some parameters here, Cameron."

"You're upset. Maybe we should talk about this later?"

"Damn well I'm upset. And what do you mean we should talk about this later? It's nearly midnight here. Do you think I'm going to sleep tonight? No, Cam, I demand an explanation."

"Nate, let me assure you, it's about me, not you. You haven't done anything."

"Then why the trial separation?"

"That's what I want to know," said another voice offscreen. Roger stepped into frame and waved. He then walked past, trailing a suitcase behind him.

"What's that for?" his employer asked.

"This small one's for you," the butler replied.

"Whatever for?"

"Because Rowena doesn't pack light."

"Where are you two going?" I asked.

"Search me," Cam replied. "Where are we going, Roger?"

"To Sydney."

"I can't go to Sydney. What about the T-shirt shop?"

"You have enough staff to run that place, and without your meddling, they may just turn a profit."

My estranged partner pouted like a kid who'd missed dessert.

"Roger's right," I said. "Our staff don't need us around."

"Great. Now my butler and my boyfriend are ganging up on me. Don't you two get it? I need some time out."

"What did you say, Cam?" I asked. "Did I hear your words right? 'My butler and *my boyfriend*'? It's nice to know I'm not yesterday's news."

"I also said I need some time out."

"Why?"

"I need to think some things through." He turned to Roger who was offscreen. "And that doesn't mean I'm going to Sydney."

His all-knowing servant entered the frame. "Listen here, young man. There's a gorgeous Australian on the other side of that webcam who has just spent six months away from home in your kingdom. And the moment his back is turned, you decide you're Greta Garbo."

"Huh?"

"You young ones have no camp sensibility." He shook his head. "Cameron, you've decided you want to be alone. Alone? Whatever for? You're in love."

"I know, but I just need to sort my head out."

"This isn't about the night I met your parents?" I asked. "Your closed lips say it all. Didn't they like me?"

"Trust me, Nate. This isn't about my parents."

"I thought your mum and I hit it off."

"Mom loved you. And so did Dad, in his *own* way."

"So what's this about?"

"I need space."

"Oh, stuff you, Cam! I miss you. And I missed you all through my long flight here. And now you pull this stunt on me? What have I done to deserve this?"

Roger pointed straight through the screen. "That man deserves more than this. That man deserves an explanation face-to-face. That's why I've booked accommodation for you, me, and your aunt Beverley!"

"Oh great," said Cameron. "I decide to do a Gretel Garbo—"

"Greta Garbo."

"Whatever. I decide I need some space, and my butler and my aunt decide I don't."

"They're right," I protested. "You're turning back into that rich kid who didn't want to share his thoughts and feelings with the one he claimed to love. Hell, Cameron, we just had six months getting to know each other. Longer, if you count Tokyo and our time here in Sydney. And now this? We spend an evening with your parents and you revert to being a spoiled brat."

"That's a low blow, Nate."

"But he's right," said Roger. "This is exactly the way you treated your charming Australian when you were trying to romance him in your vast city. He's gone for one second and you forget he's your partner. There is no *I* in team, Cameron Charlton. He deserves an explanation, and not through the internet."

"Thank you, Rog," I said.

"All right. I'll go to Sydney with you and Aunt Beverley, and explain in person why I need time out. Then I'll jump on the next plane home." Roger grinned at me through the camera. "I thought my butler was supposed to be on my side?"

"I am. That's why I'm doing this, Cameron. That's why I'm doing this."

Chapter Four

"HE'S SEEING SOMEONE else."

"Ben!"

"Why else wouldn't he want you back in a hurry?"

This was my friend's attempt at making me feel better. While I was having my earlier confrontation with my boyfriend through the laptop screen, Lucy called Ben. Ben came straight over with Fox and dragged me to a gay bar. I really wanted to stay up with Lucy and talk about my conversation with Cam, but she had to be up early to run her café. That's why she called in the troops.

Although he was a pretty boy, Fox had that well-worn look that boasted a history. His serious demeanor could turn into hijinks at any time, without care of who might get hurt. Like a thief in your apartment, watching everything carefully and ready to cause chaos if the moment called for it.

He hadn't said much. A polite hello and a few quick glances at me, while spending most of his time observing Ben. I felt I was being judged by this redhead. He was attractive and seemed to know it. An odd choice of friend.

The three of us stood at a table on what was a quiet night in town. Two guys sitting on stools found it easier to communicate on social media rather than say a word to each other. A man, who was old enough to remember when sex was illegal, sat with his beer at the bar. The barman wiped down the bench while singing along to the video jukebox.

"He's hot." Wow! The redhead spoke.

"Which one?" Ben asked.

"The barman, of course."

"Barmen are always hot," I replied. "They're manufactured at the same factory that make the dolls that give little girls complexes about the way they look."

"You should chat him up," said Ben.

"Who?" I asked. "Me?"

"No. Fox."

"Am I chatting him up for you as well, Ben?" the plus-one asked. "Is it a threesome?"

"If you can arrange it, count me in."

Fox homed in on the barman like a smart bomb. I was relieved he was out of our hair.

"You don't like him, do you, Nate?"

"What makes you say that?"

"It's written on your face."

"Well, he can hardly strike up a conversation."

"He's shy. Trust me."

"That's no reason for the armor of attitude."

Fox rested his elbow on the bar, propping his head up like he was caught in a daydream. The barman noticed and soon appreciated someone to talk to.

"There, you see? He *can* strike up a conversation."

"That's because he has sex on the brain. He's homing in on his kill."

"You'll get to like him. Believe me." Ben sounded more like a proud parent than a friend.

"So Fox is in for the long haul? He must be good in bed."

"Nathan!"

"Now that's a reaction I didn't expect. When did you become coy?"

"I'm not. He's just a fuck buddy. That's all."

We watched the king of cool and his willing victim. Then I watched Ben watch the king of cool. There was a slight smirk on my friend's face.

"Nate, why are you analyzing me?"

"I'm not analyzing."

"You're watching me like a hawk."

"I just can't tell whether you want him to succeed with the barman or not."

"What's that supposed to mean?"

"Nothing."

"Anyway, this night is about you. Not me."

"Or Fox."

"I think you're focusing on my friendship with Fox to avoid facing up to whatever is going on with Cam."

"Ben, it's a welcome distraction."

"More wine?"

"Hell, yes."

My friend meandered off. The barman didn't notice Ben until he squeezed Fox's shoulders from behind, startling his bonk buddy. They gazed at each other briefly until Ben jerked his head unnaturally to only look at the barman. *How odd.* As the bottle was being fetched, Ben only shared brief words with Fox, like he was a random he'd only just met, rather than a guy he'd been screwing the life out of. *Am I reading this right?* Ben made his way back with the wine and promptly topped up our glasses.

"Do you and Fox have some sort of code on the way you act around each other when one is picking up?"

"Huh?"

"I mean, is this a night for two rather than three? Him and the barman?"

"Nate, you're speaking in tongues. Forget Fox. What the hell happened with you and Cameron?"

"I don't bloody know. I finally meet his parents, who are not the best company, and I put on all the airs and graces. I'm the perfect boyfriend. Laughing at all the right moments. Ignoring his boorish father's snide remarks—"

"About you?"

"No. About Cameron. His dad really doesn't like how Cam doesn't have a real career."

"Can you blame him? All you guys have been doing is running that arty T-shirt place. Don't pout, Nate. You told me yourself, it isn't making much money."

"True."

"And you just admitted Cam doesn't have a real job. While you two have been living the romantic adventure, his dad has been the realist."

I opened my mouth, but no words came out. Ben was right, of course. A storybook encounter in Prague. Sleepless nights in New York. A meeting of minds in Tokyo. More romance in Barcelona. Hey, paid escorts didn't get it this good. No wonder his father was such a killjoy.

Fox and the barman were now peering at Ben like he was the last scrap of food in an apocalyptic world. Their mouths were almost dribbling. This was my cue to be invisible.

"Go on," I said.

"I can't let down a mate."

"Who? Him or me?"

"You."

"Ben. I really have nothing more to say. Until Cam and his entourage get here, I won't know what's happening. That's when I'll need a shoulder to cry on. Go bonk the barman."

He stayed seated. But then he turned his head to his left. I looked in that direction to see one of the guys who was addicted to his phone ambling toward us. Ben looked back at me with an eyebrow raised. I shook my head.

"Hey, for all you know, you could have been dumped, Nate. You might be a free agent."

"Thanks."

"No, seriously. You and Cam are taking time out. I think that gives you a hall pass."

While I tried to answer, Ben charged up to the bar to flirt. And although my curly-haired suitor was attractive, cheating was the last thing on my mind. Another bottle of wine and a fresh glass were plonked on our table by the barman. He told me Ben had paid for it. My impromptu date refilled my drink and then filled his own.

"I'm not interested in sex," I declared.

"That's the most uninspired pickup line I've ever heard. I'm Cameron."

"Cameron! Of all the names you could have had."

"Shout it from the rooftops, why don't you?"

"Sorry, Cameron. I'm Nate."

"So you're here to drown your sorrows rather than to pick up?"

"You could say that."

"Well, Nate, that's what mysterious strangers are for—to tell your troubles to."

"Um—" Suddenly this outsider seemed very charismatic. *No, Nate, no!*

"Who's the other Cameron?"

"My boyfriend who wants a trial separation."

"Why?"

"I've been asking myself that all afternoon. Why? I've been a supportive boyfriend, haven't I? I put up with his shit in the early days when he wouldn't open up to me. I molded him into a happier human being. I slaved over a hot stove to introduce him to recipes as good as those in fancy restaurants, once I learned to cook. I stayed up while he had band practice in our home, even though I really wanted to sleep. I put up with his boorish father's jibes and acted as the perfect son-in-law. Why does he need time alone? That's what I want to know. Why? Why?"

I could feel it. There was no stopping now. I choked on emotion, and it was determined to gush through my closed throat. I slammed the table with my fist several times, trying to stop the waterworks from starting.

My other Cameron opened his arms hesitantly. I clasped both his hands and pulled them around me. He looked to Ben and Fox, so I turned as well, but they were taking turns kissing the barman. Then I sobbed uncontrollably into his shoulder, leaving a snotty wet patch on his shirt.

Chapter Five

"WELL, DEAR, HOW much do you remember of that night?" Roger was quizzing me.

"I know I was the perfect son-in-law," I replied.

"See. He doesn't remember a thing," Aunt Beverley noted.

This was brunch at Lucy's café where Lucy insisted the food was on the house just so we could get to the bottom of what was going on. And with my best girl pal by my side, we dined on omelet and Turkish toast.

The spring onions added the sharp tang that made this recipe unique. Fetta also weaved itself into the delicate balance of flavors as mushrooms weighted the eggs with an earthy texture. And the crunch of the toast with home-churned butter! Yeah.

"Excuse Nate," said Lucy. "He always does this."

"I know," Roger replied. "It's like he's sharing his orgasm face out in the open, every time he eats."

"Forgive me," I said. "I can't help it if I *like* food."

"Yes, but there's liking food and wanting to roll around in a field with it," Beverley retorted.

I sipped my coffee. "How come Cam didn't come to brunch?"

"He doesn't know we're here with you," Roger replied.

"How could you not tell him? I need to see him. I really need to see him."

"Not until we get to the bottom of this."

"We're the buffer zone," Beverley added.

"The buffer from what?" Lucy asked.

Roger briefly smiled at my gal pal as if he was consoling her for losing a loved one. "Nathan, darling, tell me what you remember."

"I remember it was a comedy of errors, with Rowena coming out and spraying Cam and his mum."

"The sad fact is, I wasn't aiming at them. I was aiming at you."

"Me?"

"Yes, you! But you were so drunk you crashed on the floor, but that still didn't shut you up."

"You were blind drunk when you met Cam's parents?" Lucy needed a clearer picture.

"I was tipsy. But I wasn't drunk."

"It was really Roger's fault," said Beverley. "He admitted to me that he filled our Nathan up with endless cocktails."

"He was nervous," Roger argued. "I was just calming down the poor man before the soap opera known as Cameron's mom and dad was allowed to unfold."

"And unfold it did," I said.

"But Nate dear, you were part of that unfolding," Beverley declared.

"Can someone tell me what Nathan did that night?" Lucy asked.

"I thought it was a perfect night," I said. "We all laughed after the soda siphon mishap."

"Why was soda being sprayed?"

"Cam's mum likes to smoke indoors and Cam lets her. She singed the sofa."

"No, she didn't," said Roger.

"Yes, she did. She said so."

"No, Nate. That's their code. When they need me to diffuse a situation, they mention fire. And I try to put out that fire. You were that fire."

"No, I wasn't. Your badly aimed soda stream lifted the mood from Mr. Charlton's grumblings."

"Nate, let's hear what happened from someone who was coherent that night," said Lucy.

We all looked around. The rest of the brunch crowd were tuning in. Sheepishly, they returned to their meals. We eased into each other across the table as Roger lowered his voice.

"Cam's mom asked Nate about Elliot."

"Why?" asked Lucy.

"Because my sister is a sticky beak," Beverley replied.

"And how did you answer, Nate?"

"I said Elliot was queenier than Cameron, but he was more direct."

"And you said that the sun shone through the clouds just for him," Roger added.

"Yeah, I said that."

"And that the world would grin back as he smiled."

"Yes."

"And how that blond curl in the middle of his forehead was all you could think about when you were apart."

"I think I'm seeing the picture," said Lucy.

"Uh-huh," said Beverley. "You definitely are, sister."

"And how since he's been gone, that blond curl is the feature that keeps making you smile in times of sadness," Roger continued.

"I said that?" Clarity was not my friend.

"And how in the hours you spent in this café, he kept making you smile and kept you going, knowing that he would be back by your side when you got home."

"Well, he was the guy you wanted to spend your life with," Lucy added.

"He said that too. Then Nate went on to talk about how they were going to buy a place together, somehow. Even if it was on the outskirts, but you wanted a place that said Nathan and Elliot in every picture, piece of furniture, and feature wall."

"I did go on, didn't I?"

"And that style would include Elliot's choice of bold-colored walls, an exotic bathroom, and a separate dining area with cherry-tinted floorboards and speakers in the ceiling. Cherry-tinted floorboards? Really, Nate? Everything else I agree with, but a cherry tint?"

"Did I really say all that?"

"Yes, you said cherry tint!"

"I always knew you weren't over this Elliot guy," Beverley asserted. "And now my nephew has a broken heart."

"How do you think I feel?" I begged. "It wasn't my idea to stay apart from your nephew."

"Can you blame him? Face it, Nathan, he's not the love of your life."

"But—" I stopped myself. The words *But the love of my life is dead!* nearly left my lips.

"What were you going to say?" Roger asked.

"You're staring into space, Nathan," said Lucy.

People existed in my peripheral, including those I was sitting with. I closed my eyes. Cutlery was clattering. Conversations became an ambient murmur. Somewhere I heard food sizzling, while the bitter aroma of coffee beans being ground sharply woke my nostrils.

And with that momentary seductive shock came a vision. Elliot was across the table from me.

"How's it going, Nathan?"

"In the words of Kylie, I can't get you out of my head."

"I know. It's nice to know I'm not forgotten."

"You'll never be forgotten, Elliot. You'll be with me always. I just need to make you less of a priority."

"If we broke up like normal people, you wouldn't be in this mess."

I wanted to cry. He played with the curl on his forehead. I wanted to cry even more. So I studied the weird pastel suit and thin leather tie he was wearing.

"What's the deal with the clothes? Have you been op shopping in heaven, if that's where you are?"

His mouth skewed to the left. "Of course I'm in heaven. And it's so cool there. Dance parties. Chic restaurants. Tours of afterlife architecture. And they even have a gay angel looking after stuff."

"I'm glad to hear you've settled in."

"Don't worry about me, Nathan." He pointed at me across the table. "You have a life to lead. I've been gone for years. I'm just part of your history. I'm part of your story. But your story goes on."

"It's embarrassing to say this, Elliot, but you're making me feel dumped."

"So you've got to ask yourself why you're still pining for your dead ex, because *dumped* is probably how that American is feeling."

"His name's Cameron."

"Whatever."

"Jealous?"

He didn't answer. Instead, he waved goodbye as his image faded.

"Earth calling Nate." It was Roger's voice.

"Ground control is calling you." This time, Lucy.

"He did this before Cam's mom and dad arrived."

"That's why you filled him to the eyeballs with alcohol!" Aunt Beverley quipped.

I opened my eyes. "I'm here, guys. I'm here."

Roger yawned. Beverley covered her mouth, trying not to yawn.

"Jet lag?" Lucy asked.

"Why are you guys so far away from the States?" Beverley answered with another question.

"It's only around six p.m. back in New York," I said.

"I don't care," said Roger. "We still need to sleep off the long flight."

"And the cocktails we had on the way," Beverley added.

Our American guests stood. Lucy and I stood too.

"Dinner tonight, at our place, please," said Roger.

"How big is your hotel room?" I asked.

"Three separate bedrooms and a fully functioning kitchen," Beverley replied. "And it's not a hotel."

"It's not?"

"I didn't want to be cooped up," Roger replied. "So we hired a house in Paddington. I wanted to be close to the gay strip."

"So come over around seven," said Beverley. "We should recover from our midday nap by then. The boys can talk about boys, and us girls can talk about girls." She winked at Lucy.

"I'm not gay," my friend replied.

"You're not? With that colorful fifties dress and the scarf in your hair, you'd make a wonderful femme."

Lucy and I shared glances.

"Will Rowena be there tonight?" I asked.

"Of course, Nate. It's an occasion! Lucy has to meet her."

"My dear," said Beverley, leaning into my gal pal, "everyone has to meet Rowena. You haven't been inducted unless she makes an appearance."

"Text me the address," I said. The visitors soon departed, just after Roger asked for a lamington to take home. He was prodding it inside the paper bag and licking chocolate from his fingers. He said something about it being his cross-cultural food experience. Lucy and I went to her office the minute they'd left.

"You shouldn't daydream in the middle of a conversation, Nathan."

"I was escaping the drama of what I'd said to Cam's mother about Elliot."

"I know, but you were thinking about Elliot as well. Don't look surprised. We've been friends too long for me not to know what's going on in that anally retentive head of yours."

"I didn't realize I still missed him."

"Nate, you are always going to miss him. Hell, you were about to admit he was the love of your life in front of the butler and the aunt, just after the aunt clearly said that Cameron was not the love of your life."

"You knew?"

"I knew. That's why you shut down. We can't confirm that in front of Bev and Roger."

"I still see him. Not as a ghost at home, which would be inconvenient in Cam's New York apartment, but in my thoughts. I still see his adorable curly hair and his dreamy blue eyes. And he still makes me laugh, or at least, smile."

"And do you long to hold him?"

"Not as much as I used to. My time in New York has watered that down."

"Nathan, how can you get lost in his eyes and not still want to hold him?"

"Because I know I can't. It's a reality I had to face. It's a tortured, ugly, harsh reality I had to face."

"So you don't think of Elliot when you're making love to Cameron?"

"Lucy!"

"Just asking."

"Of course not!"

"Sorry, Nathan." She paused. "Tell me about Cam."

"He makes me laugh, but not in an Elliot way. Cam makes me laugh when he doesn't mean to. And often when he does mean to. I was watching him try to prepare canapés and he was getting food everywhere. If Roger hadn't helped him, his parents would be bundling up the creations off the plate just to keep them together. Elliot might have been a himbo, but he could throw food together."

"We're talking about Cameron, not Elliot."

"Yes, I know. Cameron. He's goofy, aloof, but sometimes very centered. He can explain a complicated concept without confusing you."

"That's nice, Nate, but how does he make you feel?"

I reflected. "Special."

"Just special?"

"Like I'm the whole world to him. Like I can't put a foot wrong. Like I'm the luckiest man alive." She seemed deep in thought. "Does that answer your question, Lucy?"

"With crystal clarity."

Chapter Six

HE GREETED ME with a half smile. I grinned from ear to ear. He swallowed as if something was caught in his throat, then turned to Lucy.

"It's nice to see you again."

"It's nice to see you again too, Cam."

"And what about me?" I asked.

His smile became warmer. "It's always nice to see you, my outspoken Australian."

I stepped forward with my arms out. He embraced me. I listened to his heavy breathing as his arms held me tighter. I clutched him, taking three short breaths as if I was going to cry. I didn't, although every part of my body was telling me to let go emotionally. To make this fool see I was in love with him. But if I was shunned, my world would crumble. So I kissed his cheek, then moved away.

At that moment, I heard Roger's alter ego burst into song, informing us that there was no business that could be topped by show business.

"Come inside," Cam said.

He walked ahead, and as Lucy followed him out from the entrance hall, I whispered, "Thank you for your support."

She stopped. "Nathan, you have me wrapped around your little finger," she whispered back.

Past the bedrooms was a grand living space. Rowena, still singing, was wearing a smart black dress with white trimming on which she had already smeared a bit of pasta sauce near her shoulder. It had missed her floral apron and was too far up for her to notice without a mirror. I knew better than to tell her about it as it would send the old girl into a tizz over what to change into.

Then Cam and Aunt Beverley joined in on the chorus of the show business song. The three stood singing for each other's entertainment, grinning like thieves.

"This is normal in New York," I said to Lucy.

"Normal in New York, or just normal in Cameron's apartment?"

"Normal wherever Rowena tends to be."

They finished the song with the cross-dressing butler attempting a high kick. Beverley found her inner Rockette, joining her partner in crime. Together they high kicked in turn until Rowena extended her leg so far, we got more than a bird's-eye view of what was hidden under that dress. At the same time, her heel shot off like a bullet. Lucy ducked, avoiding a black eye. A glass ornament behind her wasn't so lucky.

"Oh dear," said Aunt Beverley. "That's why I wear sensible shoes."

She was dressed casually tonight. Denim jeans and a checked shirt was her dining wear. There was a hanky in her right shirt pocket and another in her back pocket. I was about to ask what they represented but realized quickly I didn't want to know.

Then Rowena hummed the show business tune.

"You're not going to sing it again, are you?" Cam asked. "That will make it ten times in a row."

"Eleven," Rowena corrected. "I'm just adding a spark of gaiety to the evening."

The first verse was once again pumped out in tragic contralto. Beverley sang as well, while Cam picked up a wooden spoon from the kitchen bench and waved it around like a conductor.

Lucy and I finally picked up the words after five more renditions and added our voices to the next performance. We only got to the part about stealing an extra bow when we smelled something burning.

"Christ!" Rowena yelled. "The garlic bread!"

Smoke billowed out of the wall oven. It was as if fog was filling a disco floor and you could no longer see your dance partner. Lucy clutched onto me, while Cam disappeared somewhere in the clouds. Then I was struck by a wayward tea towel, which Bev was using to fan away the smoke. When all was clear, Rowena stood with two burnt rocks in her kitchen mitts.

"What have we learned here?" Cam asked.

"Show tunes and garlic bread don't mix," his hired help replied.

"True. Next time try the top forty."

Although we were having pasta, the dining table was set for something more formal. White plates edged with gold sat in each place. On top of each piece of dinnerware was a matching bowl and, to the sides, sat gold cutlery.

"How many courses are we having?" I asked.

"Just two," Bev replied. "But Rowena insisted on going all out."

Elaborate purple and yellow flowers with petals tinted in garlic smoke sat in two glass vases. As I studied the arrangement, I realized that with only five of us dining, this extravagance would get in the way of us seeing each other across the table.

Near the television were three large suitcases. One in fire-engine red made of sturdy metal, the other two simply black.

"You haven't unpacked?" I asked.

"Oh we have," Cam replied. "Roger's wardrobe is full."

"They're my extra outfits," Rowena proclaimed. "It is Mardi Gras season after all."

"So it is." I rubbed my chin. "How did I forget?"

"You've had a lot on your mind," Lucy replied.

There was one other addition to the dining table. Five red cocktails ready to drink.

"Shall we?" Rowena asked.

We each grabbed one. There was a strong taste of raspberry and the burning sensation of too much vodka. Lucy licked her lips after the first sip, and very quickly emptied her glass. Rowena opened the fridge where a whole tray of identical cocktails was waiting. Lucy had no hesitation in taking another glass from her hostess.

"What about work tomorrow?" I asked.

"Don't worry about it, Nate. I've gone to work hungover before."

I nodded, realizing she was right.

"Cameron, my charming American, I've missed you." These words flowed from me.

"You probably hate me," he replied.

"I don't think I hate you. I just know we have something to talk about."

"Good point," said Beverley. She pointed to the hallway. "Now go to your room, Cameron, and have a word with your man."

Cam had scored the master bedroom, complete with en suite of which a third consisted of a space with two showerheads. This was luxury, pure and simple. A bidet was also there for spoiled guests, and the whole room was covered in ceiling-high black tiles. I imagined a kinky middle-aged couple owning this. Champagne would be drunk with friends under the shower, before a private costume party would continue in the master suite.

"*I'm* sleeping on Lucy's couch at the moment. *You're* living like you always have."

"For *most* of my life. Not all of it." He smiled softly.

"Cameron, I didn't mean to go on about Elliot. I was drunk."

"And when you're drunk, you're honest. It's just human nature."

"But Elliot is the past. It's not like I can go back to him."

"But if he was here right now, alive, you'd go back to him in a heartbeat."

I looked to the king-size bed. A prop that could come in handy. I walked backward toward it, kicked off my shoes, and perched myself against the pillows. I beckoned Cam to join me.

"Really? You're thinking of sex at a time like this?"

"Sex is the last thing on my mind. The way you made me...the way I feel at the moment..." Cam looked at his feet. "See, Cameron, honesty, without the booze."

"Nate, you made me feel like the delayed rebound boyfriend. And worse, you made me feel like that in front of my parents."

"How can you call the last six months a rebound?"

"Maybe I was fooling myself. You finally showed me what love actually felt like, but that's because you had the real thing."

"Cam, join me on the bed."

He shook his head. I moved to the edge and sat with my feet on the carpet.

"A moment ago, I questioned you about Elliot. About if he was alive today, would you return to him in a heartbeat? But you had nothing to say except to invite me onto the bed."

"What can I say? If Elliot were alive today, we'd still be together. No, don't look away, Cam. Of course, we'd be together, I think. But life didn't finish up like that. Cam, look at me, please."

"I didn't think you'd be so direct."

"You know me better than that."

It's strange to say that silence filled the room, as silence is nothing, but perhaps that's just it. Nothing filled the room. A nothing that gave our thoughts too much room to echo.

In front of me was my boy. Someone I was trying to put together again. No, scrub that. Part of me was angry for being shunned and made to feel like a leper. But if this was going to get back on track, I couldn't shy away from the cards I'd dealt on the night I'd met his parents.

"Cameron, I can't take back what I said, but hell, I'm in love with you."

He met my eyes.

"Yes, I am. And we've had this great start. You've serenaded me in the early days. You showed me *your* New York like a tour guide willing to please. And we've had a couple of faux honeymoons in Tokyo and Barcelona. Not many couples have that type of start. And we've started a business."

"Not a successful one. My dad's right on that account."

"It's successful to us because it's brought us closer. We searched for artists. Approached them. One of them, we even had to flirt with—"

"Yeah, a woman."

"Sally likes gay men flirting with her. Hey, we took her out on the town. She's family now and runs the shop when we can't."

"What does that prove, Nathan?"

"That we have a relationship. We work together, and we work together well."

"But is that enough?" He sat next to me on the bed.

"It's more than many relationships have. And hell, we haven't even made a year yet. We still make love, all the time! And you know us gay men. If the passion was going to go, it would have said bye-bye at least four months ago."

"But Elliot—?"

"Cameron, please. I had a relationship. Many people older than us have second or third marriages, and they take their experience into the next one. You are not my rebound. You are my second and, if I keep playing my cards right, final long-term relationship."

A half grin returned to his face. That fearful boy had left and my charming American had returned. The sculptured mouth that had been painstakingly smoothed to perfection was waiting once more to kiss me. I tasted his lips. A delicacy I had missed. A delicacy that wasn't leaving me ever again.

"Nate, I'm sorry. I feel like an idiot putting you through this."

"At least I'm not the only drama queen in this relationship."

He looked back at the pillows. We snaked back toward them. I cushioned myself against the softest one as Cam cushioned himself against my body. We sat; my arms wrapped around my man who once again seemed familiar.

"Remember our opening night party?" he asked.

"Of the Art-Wear Shop? Of course. We had those new plastic garbage bins full of punch."

"And Sally kept filling them up with any bottle she could find. Vodka. Gin. Absinth."

"I'm sure there were chemical additives as well."

"I don't think so, Nate."

"But you're not entirely sure."

He rubbed his chin. "That might explain why Sally took her top off and—"

"—and why she was straddling that leather man and singing about riding some horse in some desert. Now, why wouldn't they give that horse a name?"

"Where did that leather man come from? Whose friend was he?"

"Who cares, Cam? They made the party an Instagram success."

"Yeah, then Brett turned up the music and led everyone in Bollywood dance moves."

"And all those moves worked well with house music."

"And while I was doing the 'Change the light bulb' move, you thought I invented something called 'Scratching a tall man under his chin.'"

"Hey, that's what it looked like, Cameron. Who rubs a light globe? Were you coaxing it out of its socket?"

"It's the way I dance, Nate!"

"I know. Then you fell into my arms as you were trying to do the Sprinkler."

"Yes, I did."

"And I wrapped my arms around you like I'm doing now."

"And we swayed to the house beat."

"As the entity known as Cam and Nate."

"And that entity stayed in bed all the next day and made love."

"Yes, we made love over and over again. Which proves my point, Cam. Sally spiked the punch with more than just alcohol. Our hangovers were delayed one extra day."

"Who cares? I enjoyed the delights of my hot Australian."

He pressed harder against me, gazing into my eyes. But his look was not one of lust. His look was of my man returned. Returned from fear. Returned from pointless jealousy.

I was about to kiss his perfect lips when Lucy stumbled into the bedroom, spilling a little of her red cocktail. "That Rowena," she began. "She's beyond wicked. And she makes fantastic cocktails."

"How many have you had?" I asked.

"Seven. No, six. Or is this number eight?"

"And the night's just begun," said Cam.

"Between Lucy and Rowena, it will be a night to remember."

"So how did everything go between you two?" she asked. "You over the Elliot thing, Cam?"

"Err, yeah."

She spun around once like a Disney princess before crashing to the floor, surprisingly without losing any of her drink. "I can understand why you'd be jealous, Cam. I mean, Elliot and Nathan were soul mates. Oh, Nathan, don't glare at me. The wind might change and your eyes will be stuck looking like Frankenstein's."

"You don't think Nate and I are soul mates?" Cam asked.

"You're something different. And I can't say I'm not jealous of you and Nate. Gawd, I'd love to be paraded around the streets of New York, or flown to Barcelona on a whim, but as for closeness—" Her eyes met Cam's. "Nate's charming American, you have charisma!"

"And Elliot didn't?"

"He had sass. He knew who he was and didn't care who else worked it out."

"I'm not sure I know what you mean."

"Shouldn't we go back the dining room?" I asked in desperation. "Dinner might be ready."

"Rowena sent me to tell you it will be ready in ten. Now where was I? Oh yes, I was talking to Cameron. Now, Cameron, Nate and Elliot were the old married couple, long before most couples I know are old married couples. And how I longed for something half as good. Instead, I was cheated on by someone I thought was the real thing. And I couldn't tell anyone. I was embarrassed. When your best gay friend is in the perfect relationship, you feel like such a failure that you can't keep yours together." I thought she chuckled. I quickly realized the tears were coming soon. She raised her cocktail. "To Nate and Elliot!"

Before the drink reached her mouth, she was sobbing like a bride abandoned on her wedding day. Cameron stood. I thought he might have been about to open a drawer, find a hanky, and offer it to her. Instead, he calmly walked to the bedroom door, stopped, observed my messy friend, and then stepped out.

Chapter Seven

"NATHAN, I AM so sorry." Lucy's words were the backdrop to my slumber. "My own stupid envy controlled my voice and...and...and that Rowena was no help with her lavish cocktails."

"Do we need to speak about this now?" I mumbled. I sunk deeper into the couch.

"Sorry, Nathan. I didn't mean to wake you. I was practicing my apology."

I opened one eye. There she was, dressed like a 1950s movie star on vacation, complete with red-framed sunglasses. Even in casuals, she had class.

"Where are you off to?"

"Work."

"Oh yeah. It's a workday. Hey. I've got a favor to ask."

"Anything, Nate."

"I need a job. Can I barista in your café?"

"I don't really need another staff member, but I'm riddled with guilt. I owe you something so it may as well be a job. Tomorrow morning?"

"I'll grind the coffee beans to aromatic perfection."

"Good. You know, Nate, you don't have to throw yourself into a job just to deal with your problems."

"That's not why I'm asking for a job."

"Okay." She turned to leave but then changed her mind. "Make yourself at home today. Ben and Fox are coming back with me tonight to cheer you up. But if you and Cam—"

That's all I heard. Sleep was tapping me on the shoulder, and I had all day to listen.

"I'VE ONLY SPOKEN to Roger today," I said. I studied a piece of fried chicken. "How many calories are in this?"

"You're on the verge of singledom and you're worried about calories?" Ben queried. "On second thought, that makes a lot of sense. You have a layer of 'happily married' fat to get rid of. Grab a wing instead."

"Thanks for the encouragement. Remind me why we're friends?"

Ben brought dinner over to Lucy's that evening. A heart-attack serving of chicken in a bucket, mashed potato, and two one-liter tubs of gourmet gelato.

"If I knew we were having this, I would have rolled a joint," said Fox. He gave an expression as if he'd shared something profound.

"This is comfort food, Nate," said Lucy. "It's what you need at the moment. And if I know you, you'll devour it as if you're performing some sexual act."

"He'll what?" Fox asked.

"He eats like he's having sex," Ben replied. "Just catch him at the right moment. Once that crispy skin leaks onto his taste buds and the crunch of marinated spices blows his mind, he'll be longing for the next sinfully succulent taste."

"That sounds smutty," I said.

Fox looked to Ben with a wicked grin. Ben's head stayed stationary as only his eyes moved sideways to stare at Fox, smirking like a choir boy with a guilty secret.

"Well, at least someone's getting sex," said Lucy. She bit into a drumstick.

"I know how you feel," I said. "I keep waking up with a hard-on for nothing."

"You didn't, you know, in my apartment when you got up?"

"No, Lucy. I hit it with a cold spoon and it magically disappeared." I poked my tongue out.

"I don't want sticky—"

"Lucy, calm down. I didn't."

"If you're that desperate, you could have had that guy that was trying to pick you up the other night," said Fox.

"If you didn't dribble all down his shirt," Ben added.

"It's so cute the way you finish each other's thoughts," I replied. I bit into a breast piece. It was succulent.

"Now, Nathan, you said you spoke to Roger today?" Lucy leaned forward as she asked this.

Ben copied her move. "Yes, I did. Beverley and Rog have convinced Cam not to fly home. But he said it took a while to sway him."

"Can I say something?" Fox asked.

"Sure."

"He sounds like a spoiled brat."

"Fox!" Lucy scolded.

"But he kinda does," Ben added.

"Ben!"

"No, it's okay," I said. "Yes, he does. And sometimes I'm racking my brains, hoping he'll stop. But then I put myself in his shoes. The shoes of someone who feels they can't compete with the dead. So without trying to, Elliot is haunting his psyche."

"Elliot haunts us all," said Ben. "Remember when he made me believe I wet the bed?"

"Yes, and you were too scared to drink water the next day."

"Or tea. Or soda. I dehydrated myself for twenty-four hours."

We chuckled, except for Fox. "How did he make you believe you pissed yourself?" he asked.

"I was at work," I began.

"But it was Ben's day off," Lucy continued. "And for some reason, he slept at Nathan and Elliot's. Why did you stay at their place, Ben?"

"Another messy night," he replied. "But you stayed sober, Nate."

"I had to work the next day. Plus, you and Elliot started without me. You were already swaying on your stools when I got to the bar."

"That's right. So somehow I made it back to Nate and Elliot's. The next morning, there was a wet patch on my sheets. And on my underwear."

"My Elliot had poured half a glass of water over Ben's crotch when he was asleep."

"Apparently Elliot threw up in the bathroom during the night, and when he went back to bed, he couldn't sleep," Lucy explained. "That's what he told me. So in typical Elliot fashion, his mind came up with his evil plan. Get Ben wet."

"Seriously, I didn't drink anything the next day. And I stripped the bed and washed the sheets out of guilt. And Elliot gave me a hairdryer to get rid of the wet patch on my underwear."

"And he was going through all our aftershave spraying the patch so it didn't smell of piss," I continued. "And the funny thing is, Ben kept telling Elliot he couldn't smell piss, but Elliot kept convincing him there was a smell. Yeah, that's how Elliot told it to me when I got home."

"And I tried to avoid Nate for days. All because of Elliot."

"Why didn't you just borrow a pair of underwear from Elliot?" Fox asked.

"He convinced me all their underwear was in the laundry basket."

"Trust Elliot," I said. I felt a tear in my eye. I closed my eyelid to keep it there, hoping to see Elliot in my memories. But he avoided me this time. He knew best. "I miss him, you know."

"We all fucking miss him," said Ben. Fox reached out for his hand. Ben squeezed tightly.

"I miss the Nate and Elliot dynamics," Lucy confessed. "Although I *am* warming to the Nate and Cam dynamics. They're different, and it doesn't make them any less."

"I wish Cam could see that," I said. "All he sees is my failure to put the dead to rest."

"Guys, it's not easy." Fox's voice was slow and measured. "I lost someone. He wasn't my lover, Nate, but he was *my* someone. And I get what this dude, Cam, must be thinking. I really do. Hey, he's going all out for you, thinking you're the one. And—"

"If you don't want to talk about it, that's okay," said Ben.

"No, it's fine. I'm just going offtrack. I'm seeing both sides. Nate, you'll never forget Elliot. He's a part of you that will always be there. Some guru guy told me that the dead stay with you, in your heart. I know it's psycho-babble, but it's that thing of being a good ancestor. Someone who is remembered fondly because we look up to them after they're gone. It's what we all want. And it's what your ex achieved. Give him that, Nate. Give him that."

Through my tears, I gave Fox the biggest smile. Then I lunged and hugged him tightly. He held me, and I felt he'd never let go.

"Mate, it sounds like you need to talk," I whispered.

"One tragic dead friend story at a time."

I'm not sure how much time passed. I gather it wasn't long, but in Fox's arms, I felt some of the pain subside. And that in itself felt like a slow process.

"Sorry, Fox. I should let go of you."

"No rush, Nate. I kinda need this hug as much as you do."

I heard Lucy exhale, sensing the approval that only a woman can give. Letting you know your feelings are intact. That your breakdown is normal. That you'll get through this with dignity and grace.

I let go of Fox. Ben crawled toward him and wrapped his arms around his waist. He kissed him on the cheek in slow-motion.

I looked to Lucy but said nothing. Her face was a blank canvas, and I suspected a second round of envy as she watched the dawn of new love.

"I know what you're thinking, Nate," said Ben.

"We're just friends," Fox added.

"Friends with benefits."

"And they're pretty cool benefits." Fox purred.

"More chicken anyone?" Lucy asked, holding a piece too large not to have had hormones encourage its growth spurt. I took the genetically modified portion from her.

"So, Nate, which story do you want to hear?" Fox asked. "My tale of loss or my tale of not understanding my lover?"

"Are you sure you want to talk about this?" Ben queried.

"Your friends are my friends. No secrets here."

"Ben's right," I said. "We're making this night morbid."

"I'll tell you my 'not getting my lover' story. It will put Cam in perspective."

"No, Fox," said Lucy. "Tell him your tale of loss. We really need to shake Elliot's ghost once and for all."

Ben gave Fox one last concerned glance. Fox nodded deliberately and grinned gently like a son about to leave home convincing his mother that all will be okay in the big bad world.

"I called him Phantom. He called me Snake. Don't ask. It's a long story. But Phantom was the guy no one noticed in a crowd. The guy trying to be liked, even though anyone who took the time to know him had a soft spot for him. And I'm so glad I took that time."

"Did you—?" Ben asked.

Fox shook his head.

"Trust you to kill the mood," said Lucy.

"It's a fair question."

"It's a fair *Ben* question. Go on, Fox. Continue."

"I mean, what can I say? We drank. We got drunk. We went to the movies. He took me to the theatre. We became mates! And for the life of me, I could never get him laid."

"Straight, huh?" I asked.

"Yep. And if I'm honest to myself, I kinda made him my project. And part of that, as I said, was trying to get him laid. But he was too busy getting infatuated with my girlfriends. If he met you, Lucy, you'd be getting flowers and taken out on nervous dates. You were his type. Arty. Intelligent. Your own woman. And that was the problem. My friends saw him as a little brother, not the stud he wanted to be."

"Your eyes light up when you talk about him." Ben made this quiet observation. "It's nice."

"If you two aren't a couple by next month—" I began.

"Just friends," the two said in unison.

"Go on, Fox," Lucy said, adding a huff as an exclamation mark.

"It was the spookiest thing. We had been out somewhere, but I don't remember where. And I had to go and see this guy I started dating, and Phantom said goodbye." Fox shivered, as if someone walked on his grave. "I'm not making sense. Right, you see it was Sunday night, and I had to go and see this guy I was dating, so I told Phantom I had to go. You see, Phantom said goodbye, which was not like him."

"Fox, slow down." Ben spoke calmly. "Take a breath. Think it through. Tell the story."

This time Lucy met my eyes. We both let nothing show. But Ben raised a brow while shooting his gaze back and forth between us.

"Every time Phantom and I said our goodbyes, it was never goodbye. It was Phantom reminding me of our catch up the next week. He never said goodbye. But on this night, he did. I laughed and reminded him that our next catch up was a movie on Tuesday night. Then I hugged him. You see, I hugged him every time I left him, and this was supposed to be—"

"It's okay," said Ben. "Take your time."

Fox took the longest breath. "I hugged him and something inside was telling me not to let go. To grab a bottle of vodka and sit with him all night and talk until our tongues were numb. To sleep over in a drunken stupor. To share the bed with my straight mate and let him know I was there for him, always. But I let go. I had to meet up with a guy who lasted as long as most gay flings do. I had to fulfill my sense of duty. The next day, he had a blood clot. Of all the stupid causes of death, a blood clot! On Tuesday, his brother rang me. I didn't want to believe he was gone. And it kills me that the guy I was dating led to nothing, yet the guy who was my friend was in second place that night."

"It's hard when it just happens," I said. "They're here, then they're not."

"And you try to cry, but the disbelief stops you. Crying makes it real. You don't want that. Disbelief is the zone where everything is as it was." He licked his bottom lip, then half smiled at me. "You see, Nate, I'm not just an attitude queen."

"I never thought you were."

This time, Fox and Ben shared a glance, like soap opera actors just before announcing a twist in the plot.

"The chicken's gone cold," said Lucy.

"A sudden change of subject," I noted.

"You're right."

"Yes, you're good at sending us crashing back to earth."

"Umm," Fox began. We looked at him, encouraging him to continue. "Forget it. It's nothing."

"Go on," said Lucy.

Artoo-Detoo interrupted, letting me know I had a notification on my phone. I checked the message. It was from Cameron.

Are you up for brunch tomorrow?

I rang back. "I'm making coffees in Lucy's café tomorrow morning."

"Lunch, then?" Cam sounded lost.

"Nathan," Lucy interrupted. "Skip the coffees. I'll make them. See Cameron."

"No," I replied. "I'm sticking to my guns on this. I'm working for you while I'm in Sydney, however long that may be."

"Nate, you don't have to." This was Cam. "I can look after you while—"

"While what, Cameron? While you leave me hanging on a string?" My voice did not rise. I was proud of myself.

"No, you're right, Nathan. You're your own person. What time do you finish work?"

"What time do you want me there until?" I asked Lucy.

"Is midday okay?"

"Midday," I replied.

"I'll pick you up from Lucy's café."

"Okay."

"I love you, Nate."

"Yeah, I've heard."

The silence was deafening. "Okay, Nate. See you tomorrow."

"Bye."
"Bye."
I hung up.
"Did he say 'I love you'?" Ben asked.
I nodded.
"How do you feel?" Lucy asked.
"Like a guy who's over the bullshit."

Chapter Eight

I DIDN'T WANT to wake Lucy, so I crept out of the shower the next morning. But as I made my way to the kitchen, there she was with two cups of coffee.

"What are you doing up?" I asked. "I thought you weren't going in until later."

"I'm not."

"But it's five in the morning! Go back to bed."

"If I go back to bed, who'll drink this second cup of coffee?"

"Lucy, I have a train to catch."

"Then you'll miss that one. There's still another in fifteen minutes. It won't make you late."

I slumped on one of her kitchen stools and sipped.

"I noticed Fox won you over."

"What do you mean?"

"You thought he was a himbo."

"No, I didn't."

"Nathan, I could tell."

"Okay. I didn't like his attitude the first time I met him."

"And now?"

"Now he seems *human*." I was about to take another mouthful of coffee, but stopped. "What do you think of him?"

"Ben's keen on him."

"That's not what I asked, Lucy."

She stretched, raising her arms to touch the sky. "But I think that's the point. It doesn't matter what we think of him; he's here to stay." Her last word turned into a yawn.

"Ben won't admit that."

"He doesn't have to. We both see it."

I chuckled. "When did you feel the same way about Cameron?"

She stared out the window. "When you started posting pictures of things you liked about New York. That, my friend, was when I knew I lost you to the Big Apple, and that Cam was the real deal."

Her eyes came back to me, looking through me as if her own future was somehow written behind my physical form.

I CAUGHT A glimpse of others watching me on the platform. I searched into the distance for my train, expecting it to magically appear just because I was peering down the tracks. But it wasn't due for three minutes. And some of the others pointed to the electronic timetable above to alert me of this fact.

In Manhattan, this would've been normal. Everyone would expect the carriages to arrive early just by willing them into existence. The collective wizardry of New Yorkers.

I kept the tracks in view while thinking of the time I jumped into the front seat of a yellow cab. Cam called out to me as he hopped in the back, and at that moment, every taxi scene from every Hollywood flick I'd ever seen flashed before me. In none of them had a passenger sat in the front seat.

I turned to the cabbie and apologized, saying, "I'm Australian. It's just what we do." Ssince then, when I'm traveling alone among the skyscrapers, I chat with the driver from the passenger seat.

My train arrived. It screeched like a parakeet with a sore throat as it stopped. I got on, noticing the other weary travelers, and as I sauntered to one of the many available seats, my mind returned to Manhattan.

There was one day Cameron dragged me to a place on Houston Street. He kept saying this weird word, like he was sneezing. Knish. I repeated it, but he decided he wasn't going to give me an explanation. I just had to try one.

I bit into the crisp pastry. Inside, spinach was waiting, and as its sweetly sharp flavor ravished my tongue, a squirt of mustard rushed in. And it worked! Mustard and spinach. This unholy combination found peace on my taste buds.

Then Cam tempted me with cream cheese and cherry, which began my dedication to this ruby-red fruit. Australia doesn't do cherries. It does mangos, pawpaw, pineapple, and anything else tropical. Cherries come and go at Christmas.

As the custard-like filling slid into my mouth, I swore my allegiance to these fleshy balls of deliciousness. And whether these spherical delights were juiced, baked in a pie, swirled in vanilla ice cream, or waiting for me in the crisp casing of a knish, I was loyal to however they wanted to satisfy my desire for dessert.

Did they just announce my stop? They had. It would be a morning with the espresso line customers all reaching out like the dead waiting to be reborn. But I had to do this. I had to do this for me and Cameron.

"TO BE HONEST, Cam, I feel like breakfast." My bloodshot eyes studied the menu.

"Didn't you eat at the café?"

"I snacked on macadamia cookies. I've been running on sugar all morning."

My charming American ex, or non-ex, or whatever we were at that moment, picked me up in a taxi, opening the door while still in the backseat. I ditched my apron and entered his lair. He did, however, politely call out to Lucy to say hi. She waved back with a mega-grin.

And now we were sitting at a restaurant with pressed linen tablecloths, staff in tailored uniforms, and imported sparkling water on the table.

"Maybe we should have had dinner," I mused.

"Why?"

"We could have got drunk and let loose on how we feel."

"This place is licensed."

"No, Cameron. I need to work tomorrow morning."

"But *you're* the one who mentioned alcohol."

"Yeah, I guess I did, didn't I?"

"One glass of wine?"

"I want scrambled eggs on toast. Orange juice would be better."

"How about a dash of orange juice in your wine?"

"If you ask for orange juice with wine in this place, their disproving stares will kill us."

"Then we'll have a glass of champagne, Nate. A champagne breakfast. I'll have something with bacon."

We ordered. The ponytailed waitress fussed over my cutlery, making sure it was placed just right, and waved my napkin over my lap like it was a bedspread that needed to be straightened. Our long-stemmed glasses fizzed with the tempting sound of something my brain desperately needed: an alcoholic aspirin to numb the battleground of emotions I had for Cameron Charlton.

"A toast to—" he began.

"You were going to say 'to us,' weren't you?"

"A toast to sorting this out."

I sipped, but it seemed like the longest sip of my life.

"Cameron, to be honest, I'm getting over it."

"Over what?"

"Over having my life on hold so you can finish your tantrum…"

"Tantrum?"

"Let me finish. Your *issue*. The reason you want some time out. And I totally get that you were upset about something I said the night I met your parents, but really, kicking me out with nowhere to live? I could have moved into the spare bedroom or something while we worked things out."

"Is that how you see it, Nate?"

"Okay, I've tainted it with sarcasm, but I've been up since sparrow's fart, and I'm not the nicest person when I haven't had enough sleep. You know that."

"Is that supposed to be an apology?"

"An apology for what? I'm just being honest. Deal with it."

My eggs arrived. The waitress cranked the pepper. The flakes wafted down to meet my meal like light rain. The bubbles in my morning pick-me-up shot through my veins like caffeine. It was this instant I knew I was paying too much attention to my food and not to the reason I was sharing a meal with my distant boyfriend.

"Nate, let me say something. And hear me out. I want to get this off my chest." He cleared his throat as if he was about to address the United Nations. "I met this guy in Prague, and I knew there was an attraction. I didn't know how far it would go, but I took the risk and found out. And hell, I'm glad I did.

"We did Tokyo. We did Barcelona. And we keep doing Sydney and New York. And little by little, we started a business. It's not the greatest success. Okay, stop looking at me like that. It's not a success at all. But it's a lot of fun. We're having fun running it. And one day, that label will take off.

"Anyway, back to us. I wanted the perfect life. And that life seems perfect when *you're* in it, Mr. Nathan Jones. And I thought we were on the same page, and that Elliot— No, Nate, don't roll your eyes. Elliot is the silent cast member in this."

I sunk into my chair. Cam continued to speak.

"I know he was a big part of your life, and I thought that chapter was over, but on the night of my parents' visit, he wasn't the silent cast member anymore."

"You're jealous of a dead person."

"If you want to put it that way, yes, I'm jealous of Elliot."

"Is everything all right, sirs?" the waitress asked.

"We'll keep it down," I replied. "I'm sorry."

She gave a goofy smile and left. The sound of cutlery clanking on plates was almost deafening, as the other patrons quickly returned to their meals at the same time.

"Cameron, Elliot was part of my life, and I'm sorry if I talked about him in front of your parents, but your mum asked about him."

"And you told her about him. And told her. And told her." He chuckled. "Nate, the crux of it is, you've got me wrapped around your little finger, but I think Elliot has you wrapped around his."

"No, Cam, the crux of it is you're jealous over my dead ex, and you shouldn't be. And we could've talked about it before I flew back to Sydney. But now we've had a drama across the continents. And the world has stopped spinning for Nathan and Cameron!"

"Is that how you feel, Nathan?"

"I really don't know how I feel. No, scrub that. I know exactly how I feel. I feel like I can't make this right. That my past can't be erased, and any hint that Elliot ever happened is going to keep popping up time and time again. And I can't be sorry for that."

The waitress was on her way back, so I shut up. Cam ate silently. The bacon crunched in his mouth, which again made me realize I was paying too much attention to the small details.

"I love you, Nate."

"I love you too, but I can't be blamed for my past."

"And I'm sorry for telling you not to come back from Sydney. I should have talked about it the next day, but I didn't know how to bring it up."

"But that's always been the problem, Cam. You don't scream the house down. You keep everything stagnant as you brew over whatever it is *I've* done wrong. And this time, I was an ocean away before I even knew, yet again, that something was *my* fault!"

Chapter Nine

"I DIDN'T EXPECT this," said Rowena.

"Expect what?" I asked.

"Diplomatic tensions between Australia and the US."

She did have an air of grace as she said this, her hand wafting over her forehead as if she was going to salute me. Lucy laughed.

Rowena wore a summer dress, light and cheery, although pink was definitely not her color, even with her blonde beehive wig. Lucy, however, did suit pink in a dress just as cheery. This was their Fair Day wear, and around us this Mardi Gras tradition was in full swing.

Muscle men sweated it out in a tug of war with large crowds snapping photos for prosperity. Lesbians marched their canine buddies down a catwalk for the judges at the dog show. Food stalls sold any international cuisine you could imagine. And several dozen drag queens strutted past, making me notice Rowena's silent envy at their glamour.

It was early afternoon, and I just arrived after a morning of coffee making in Lucy's café.

"Where are the others?" I asked.

"Ben and Fox are here, somewhere," Lucy replied.

"They're probably watching the Muscle Marys tug their rope," Rowena added.

"Are they walking hand in hand?" I asked.

"Practically."

"And Cameron and Beverley *were* here," Lucy informed me. "But they've gone to see some art exhibit."

I tried to swallow the lump in my throat, but my friend's sympathetic smiles let me know I failed.

"Do they sell drinks here?" I asked. "You know, the ones with vodka?"

Lucy pointed to a small marquee with garden tables and chairs and a group of swaying people who either looked like they should go home or hadn't been home since last night.

"We can sit in there and chat," said Lucy.

"No," I replied. "We're here at Fair Day. There're guys to perv at."

Rowena offered to buy our beverages, but Lucy insisted we wait as she got in line. So my cross-dressing buddy and I studied the multicolored masses before she spoke quietly in Roger's voice.

"Nate, I've wanted to say this to you for a long time, and somehow, now that I'm in your country, it's easier for me to say."

"What is it?"

"You don't treat me like a butler, and I appreciate that."

"Cameron doesn't either."

"Hmm."

"What? You think he does?"

"He's more of a friend to Rowena than Roger. That's why I dress up a lot."

I was speechless.

"You agree, don't you? Now that you're thinking about it. It's okay, Nate. We both know Cameron is spoiled. But you've been good for him. He just needs to know it."

"It's not his fault. He's right. I'm still stuck on Elliot."

"No, you're not. If you were, you would never have moved in with us."

"Perhaps I was running away."

"No, you weren't. Trust me. I know you better than you think."

Lucy returned, balancing three drinks between her fingers. Touches of crimson nail polish shot up between the plastic cups.

"Thank you, my dear," said Rowena, amplifying her feminine tones.

"Were you discussing Cameron while I was in line?"

"Not really. I was saying what a breath of fresh air Nathan is to New York."

"I am?" I stood up straight with comic pride, then took my drink from Lucy.

"You've made Cam stop stocking up on junk food. You've learned all those fancy dishes off the internet, kicking me out of the kitchen. And you've made our home fun, romantic, carefree, and just that little bit Australian."

"How?"

"You say tom-ah-to, we say tom-ay-to."

"You say a bowl of chili, we say chili con carne."

"You say 'Where's Wally?' We say 'Where's Waldo?'"

"I get it," Lucy butted in. "You can stop now."

We wandered toward a giant slippery sheet spread over a small mound. People were being coated in lubricant to speed down the plastic plaything.

"I dare you," said Rowena to both of us.

"Not with vodka in my hand," I replied.

"After your vodka, then," Lucy said. "I'm game if you are."

I smirked unintentionally.

"That's how I like to see my Nathan. Smiling."

"I guess I should smile more." I bit my bottom lip, but I couldn't stop the rush of emotion shooting up to my throat.

Rowena passed her drink to Lucy, then spread her arms wide. "Come here, little man."

"I don't know what's come over me. I didn't mean to bring the mood down."

"Just come here for a cuddle. Every gay guy needs his girlfriends."

I buried myself in the pink summer dress. Arms the size of a sailor's wrapped around me. I didn't cry. But while people shrieked as they glided down the slide and as lube splatted against the back of my legs, I found peace in someone who was an expert in looking after my interests.

Over Rowena's shoulder, I could see Lucy. She winked, quietly sipping from both cups and making me grin at her sneaky antics. But when others strolling behind her took discreet glances at my uncertain state, I became self-conscious and pulled away.

"Are you okay?" Rowena asked.

"I think I'm just tired from the early mornings in Lucy's café."

"Nonsense. If I know you, Nathan Jones, you're pretending this drama isn't getting to you."

Lucy was nodding, agreeing with every word.

"Of course it's getting to you. And trust me, you and Cam aren't splitting up if I have anything to say about it," Rowena said.

"How can I reason with him? He's transfixed on Elliot."

"The same way you reason with all men. Make them feel like they're number one. Make them feel that no one else matters. The male ego is a fragile thing."

"Listen to us women," Lucy added. "Men want your attention all the time, unless they want time out. But when they're after your attention again, they butt into whatever you're doing so that they can feel important."

"Listen to her, Nathan. She's absolutely right."

"I'm stuck in the middle of the mutual admiration society," I joked.

Lucy shushed me, then continued. "Men need the spotlight, then they need to retreat. Then they need the spotlight again. They run around in circles in two states of play. Being important in your eyes, and being important in their own minds. And the second state of being fuels the first."

"So you talked about Elliot for longer than your allotted time. Cameron felt unimportant. The man couldn't deal with the fact that you had a past. And like all men who finally come to terms with the fact that their other half wasn't purposely built for them the day they met, your fussy American wanted to erase the software of your former self."

"But Rowena, even you knew I was talking about my ex too much," I said. "You tried to hose me down with a soda siphon."

"Yes, I did. But like all men, my employer has an overblown sense of self-importance, and the minute things weren't going his way, he kicked you out of the castle."

"I appreciate what you're trying to say, but don't you think Cam's actions show an underdeveloped sense of self-importance? Otherwise, we would have cleared up the Elliot thing before I left for Sydney."

"My Nathan," said Lucy. "You're still the realist."

"And a kindhearted one," Rowena alleged. "Regardless of what you think, his approach to this was cowardly. And I didn't drag that sulking mess here to Sydney so he could avoid you. I want closure."

"He didn't avoid me. He tried to talk to me yesterday over a fancy meal. I'm the one that was sulking."

"Delayed reaction," said Lucy. "I know you. You keep your feelings locked inside, playing it cool, until catalyst Cam let them out."

"You're both *kind* of right. The fact that he left me hanging, not knowing if I was returning to Manhattan, annoyed me. But I shouldn't have said anything over lunch. It was bad timing."

"But what would it achieve if you didn't tell him?" Rowena asked. "The way he left you wondering if you still had a relationship would have reared its ugly head at some point down the track. You would have blurted it out the next time you argued. It's good that you brought it up while it was on your mind, rather than after you kiss and make up, my dear."

"If we kiss and make up?"

Ben and Fox were ambling our way. Their gazes stayed glued on each other, hardly ever watching where they were going. One lesbian weaved her dog away from their path. They didn't notice. As they got closer, Ben waved a cylinder in the air.

"They're like two jigsaw pieces waiting to be merged," I murmured.

"I can hear wedding bells," Rowena countered.

"At least that's one relationship going somewhere."

Lucy bitch-slapped my shoulder in response to my sorry-assed negativity.

"What's in your hand?" she yelled.

"Clone-a-willy," Fox called back on Ben's behalf.

"They're talking as one," I muttered. "Some evil scientist has melded their brains together."

"Clone a what?" Rowena shouted, sounding more like Roger than his female self.

Ben threw me the cylinder. There in bold letters was what Fox said—Clone-a-Willy.

"What's it do?" I asked.

"It's a dildo maker," said Ben.

"You model it around a real penis," Fox added.

"So which one of you is supplying the penis?" Lucy asked.

"Well, I know Ben is versatile," I said. "So it *could* be Ben." I scratched my chin theatrically and looked his redhead buddy up and down. "Fox, are you a bottom?"

"I'm the cock model," Ben replied.

"Today, it's a dildo maker," said Rowena. "Tomorrow, it will be matching cock rings. Then they'll pass the 'we're just friends' phase and shop for wedding bands."

"We *are* just friends," Ben insisted.

"Yeah. And the pope is a Satanist."

"Seriously, guys," Fox said. "It's friendship with a bit of sex on the side."

Rowena, Lucy, and I all nodded slowly, with matching glazed expressions.

"We're being judged by zombies, Ben."

"None of them are getting laid at the moment. They're just jealous."

"The closest they can get to sex is standing near a puddle of lube."

"Come on, Fox, you're more than just friends with benefits." I put it out there.

His response was simple. He tackled me onto the sheet of lube, just missing some slippery bodies. The gunk covered my back and my arms while he took a handful of the stuff and rubbed it in my hair as if it were gel. I reached behind me, feeling the stuff squelch between my fingers. Slap! His cheek was glistening. I rubbed the goo over his face.

We quickly got up and joined the line, waiting to slide. Volunteers squirted the gloppy mess over us as Fox and I made sure we were covered in it. Ben joined us. We took a bottle each and squirted him as he stood with his eyes and mouth shut.

In no time, I glided. Awash with the sticky stuff, I relished in the moment. A sense of relief and of goddamned fun. I slid, like laundry down a chute, as droplets coated my thighs and my crotch. I chuckled, and somehow the tasteless gunk jumped into my mouth. As I landed on my feet, I raised an eyebrow at Lucy. She knew I was coming to get her and that she was next.

Chapter Ten

"THERE'S SOMETHING ABOUT being covered in lube that puts you in the right mood to clone a willy," said Ben.

"Well, there's a cue for polite conversation," said Lucy. "Now we just need cucumber sandwiches and a pot of tea."

It was several hours since we left the Mardi Gras fair. Lucy and I showered at Rowena's holiday home, and Ben and Fox had just arrived after going back to Ben's first to do what it was those two were compelled to do—make a dildo.

Rowena had also showered, throwing off the elaborate alter ego for Roger's return. The butler was in the kitchen, chopping onions for homemade pizzas. We had all been invited for a sleepover as there were a few extra bedrooms. Although I declined at first, insisting I had to get up early to make coffee at the café, it was Lucy who encouraged me to accept the invitation. After all, she would also have to drag herself out of bed for the breakfast shift. We'd both suffer together.

"Did you bring the dildo with you?" Roger asked.

"No," said Fox. "The silicone has to dry overnight."

Ben had a sheepish grin.

"You didn't, did you?"

"It's in my backpack. I wanted to show off our handiwork."

"But it's not dry!"

"Don't worry, I didn't bring the one we just made. I brought the one we made a couple of days ago."

"Great. Now your friends will know what *my* cock looks like."

"Fox, half of Sydney knows what your cock looks like."

"Wow. A matching set!" I replied. "And you two claim you aren't a couple?"

"I'm not going to answer that," Ben informed me.

"You guys are professional cock makers. Seriously, how can you say you aren't a couple?"

"Well, pull it out!" Roger was eager to see their achievement. He continued to cut onions as my friend hauled the dildo out of his backpack. "Ouch!"

"That's what Ben will say when I use it on him," Fox bragged.

"No, ouch! I cut my finger." He looked to his hand, then back to what our friends had created. I sprung to the kitchen and wrapped his pointer in a tea towel, as Lucy searched the bathroom for Band-Aids. Soon she was back and we played nurse.

"It's nice to be waited on," he said. "Ow. Careful."

"It's just a nick," Lucy said.

"Yes, but these hands are precious! Don't look at me like that. You don't know the adventures these hands have had. They've sautéed countless meals for gentleman callers. They've sewn sequins for daring dresses that have turned heads—"

"Yes, the other way," I interrupted.

"Dear, there's art in these hands." He extended his arm, waving his fingers in front of the kitchen window. "Look at them, Nate. Look at them! You too, Lucy. These hands have toiled like tiny communist workers. Never expecting fame. Never expecting a reward."

Ben marched over with the dildo balanced on his open hand. "And the Oscar goes to—"

With a bloodied tea towel in the sink, an older man swooning over the attention he was getting, and a glowing red phallus on display for the world to see, Cameron and Aunt Beverley picked that very moment to come home.

"It's just like being at your apartment, Cameron," the witty lesbian stated.

"This is what's wrong with your relationship, guys," said Ben. His gaze darted between Cam and I. "You need to clone a willy!"

"He may have a point," I replied.

"Which one of us would model?" Cam asked.

"Now we know," said Beverley. "They're both versatile."

She strolled to the kitchen to inspect the dildo, then pointed at Fox's crotch.

"How did you know?" he asked.

"I'm not sure. There's something about its width that reminds me of you. Kind of roguish. Carefree. A cock that leaves an impression. Like you do."

"Does it leave an impression, Ben?" Lucy asked.

He stared like a cat who was not going to make it across the road alive.

"Ben, it's not like you to be speechless," I added. "Speak up, mate. We all want to know."

"It has its unique qualities," he replied, almost choking on the words.

"What about in...?" Roger pointed to his open mouth. "Too wide? Just perfect?"

Aunt Beverley took the dildo from Ben for closer inspection. "It's too wide for me, at least from what I remember when I was a confused young woman."

"Too wide for Mama Bear. But for Baby Bear Ben, it's just right."

"I'm glad my cock is providing so much entertainment," Fox grumbled.

"Is it, Ben?" Lucy asked. "Does Fox's cock provide entertainment?"

I took it from Bev. "You know, Cam, we should do this."

He smiled at me. It was a connected smile. One I hadn't seen since New York.

"I'm game if you are," he replied.

He strolled over and scrutinized it. "Fox, was it hard to keep an erection? How did you keep it hard while Ben made the mold?"

"He kept kissing me when I told him it was going down."

"A lot of kisses, Ben?" Lucy asked.

"Yes, Miss Nosey Parker, a lot of kisses," Ben replied.

"What if we try it?" I asked. I thrust it in the air between Cam and I.

"That would be creepy."

"Creepy because we're using your sex toy?" Cam asked. "Or creepy because it would be like sharing your boyfriend?"

"Cameron, now *you're* mocking us!" Ben grumbled. "As Lucy and Nathan know, I don't *do* boyfriends. I do fuck buddies, one-night stands, and the occasional sauna. But as for boyfriends, I leave that for Lucy or Nathan." He chucked the dildo down on the bench. "You see, Cameron, I'm learning about love from my friend's mistakes. Even those mistakes that are so minor you wonder why they're even a problem. So please, forgive Nathan. If you want to see Fox and me together, then teach me that love is all they say it is."

"I think it's cocktail time," Roger announced, sounding very much like Rowena.

"HE PUT ME in my place," Cam said.

"He put you in your place half an hour ago," I replied.

"You know me, Nate. I'm never the first one to admit I'm wrong."

"We were *all* poking fun at the Ben and Fox relationship denial. We're all to blame."

Cameron and I finished our third cocktail, or at least I thought it was our third. Maybe, our fourth? The empty glasses sat on the side table in his bedroom while we sat on the floor, talking about almost everything. Everything except what we came in to talk about.

He filled me in on the various art exhibits he had seen that day and how bored Aunt Beverley was before she rolled a joint. Everything took on a new slant from then on.

I told him about the tug of war and the lube slide at Fair Day, and of Rowena's unspoken sadness at not matching the glamour of the drag queens.

And we scrutinized Ben and Fox, often stopping before any real conclusions were made about the state of their friendship. Our conversation was like ice skating. We kept our balance, sliding along with ease until any hint of crashing into something real, like discussing if we were still in love, stopped us in our tracks.

"So have you kissed and made up?" Aunt Beverley entered with a tray of martinis, each glass topped with a mouth-watering green olive. "Ah, your faces say it all. Cameron, you look like a deer in the headlights, and Nathan, you look constipated."

"Thanks for the drinks, Bev," I said. "Do you have a spare joint?"

"Not for you two. You might end up having sex, resolving nothing."

The tartness of the martini blasted the sweetness of the last drink from my tongue.

"Rocket fuel?" Cam asked.

"It might cut through the bullshit," I joked.

He smiled.

"As I'm your aunt, Cameron, I have a right to be nosy. Have you resolved *anything*?"

We both shook our heads. She joined us on the carpet, slowly easing her heavy frame with her arm as an anchor.

"Did I ever tell you about Addison?"

"In passing," Cam replied.

"Who's Addison?" I asked.

"Someone I should have chased after." She paused, subconsciously licking her lips as if remembering some salacious sex act. "Nathan, I was twenty-three, and she was a couple of years older, but man, she was everything I wasn't. Graceful. Beautiful. Feminine."

"You're graceful and beautiful, Bev."

"That's how she described me, but I never saw it. Still, what she said about me made me feel like a queen. Seriously, it did. She kept calling me her majestic woman."

"It kind of makes sense."

"We did goofy stuff together. Watched every Russ Meyer movie we could find in the video store. Marched in every protest we knew about. Tried every herbal tea on the market. Yeah, yeah, we matched the stereotype, and we matched it proudly. She convinced me to wear her costume jewelry, and I took a liking to her auburn-toned fake stone necklace."

"It would have matched your eyes."

"It did. That's why she insisted. That and the hippie leather thing she wrapped around my ankle." Beverley paused and stirred her martini. "So for three months, we made love like amphetamine-injected rabbits."

"Amphetamine-injected rabbits?"

"Hey, it's the best metaphor I can come up with after drinking Roger's cocktails. Work with me, Nate."

"You bumped uglies like carrot munchers."

"See, you can't think of anything better. Anyway, after three months, she left. No warning that there was anything wrong, and when I spoke to her on the phone, she was crying more than me. But she couldn't tell me why she left. I didn't know if she was married and her long-lost husband had returned, or if she would be cut out of a will for being a dyke, or if she was a visiting alien and her spaceship was arriving to bring her home."

"Did you ever find out why?" I looked to Cam. He shared a tender smile.

"My aunt was left in limbo, never knowing how to feel."

"I get the heartbreak, Beverley, but I'm not sure I get your point. Cam doesn't want to break off with me. Do you, Cam? Oh shit, is this what this is about?"

"No, Nate, I don't want to break off with you. My aunt is reminding me not to leave this in limbo. Otherwise people eventually move on if there's no closure, and nothing can be repaired. It's *my* cautionary tale, isn't it?"

She nodded sagely. "I saw Addison years later at a restaurant with a group of friends. She didn't know where to look, and before my dining partner convinced me to talk to her, she vanished. Exited through the kitchen, I think. Who knows? But I felt nothing. It haunted her, not me. I moved on, and she was the one in limbo."

"I need to use the bathroom," said Cam.

"Lovers who drift apart always wonder what might have been."

"Noted, Aunty, and I promise to explain what's going on." He looked at me like a kid who broke his mum's vase. "Nate, I just need to pick the right moment to talk." He quickly exited, taking his drink with him.

"What's going on?" I asked his aunt. "There's more to this than I realize, isn't there? It's not just about me carrying on about Elliot in front of his parents?"

"That's for him to answer."

"You've got to tell me. Please, Bev. Why can't he tell me?"

"Calm down, Nathan. It's nothing serious. You know what he's like. He doesn't communicate until there's been weeks of soul-searching. And I know my nephew. He'll stew over what I've said as he takes a piss, then come back here and explain everything."

"He doesn't love me anymore."

"Oh he loves you. He's just working out that a relationship doesn't come with an instruction manual. Now, Nate, before you start crying into your martini, I need to know something."

I nodded.

"Why are you working?"

"What kind of question is that? I need the money?"

"For what? Cameron hasn't frozen your access to his account."

"But it's *his* account."

"Nate, if he wasn't related to me, I'd tell you to bleed him dry for being such a drama queen."

"Bev, I don't know where I stand. And I want to surprise him."

"With what?"

"A trip to Asia. I want to go on an adventure to sort out our differences."

"An adventure? Sweetheart, you need romance. What about Paris? No, forget that. Buenos Aires!"

"Buenos Aires? Why Buenos Aires?"

"It's romance *and* an adventure."

"I can't afford it, at least not in the timeframe I'm thinking of."

"I'll fund it."

"I can't let you do that."

"Nonsense. I like you, Nathan. I like what you've done for my nephew. And as far as I'm concerned, you're part of the family. So take the money, or I'll clip you behind the ear!"

"I can't."

"Well, I'll just have to buy the tickets."

"But—"

"Another drink?" asked Fox. He entered the bedroom with a tray of tall glasses filled with something yellow.

"That's virtually iridescent," I said.

"Turn off the lights and let's see."

"What's going on out there?" Beverley asked. "Is Roger Rowena yet?"

"No, but he threatened to strip off and wear nothing but his apron. Fortunately, Lucy stopped him. Whether she's won the war remains to be seen."

"What's Ben doing?" I asked.

"Choosing music with Cameron from Roger's laptop and checking out the porn sites in his browser history. All I'll say is that he has a fascination for painted toenails."

"Why aren't you with them?" Beverley asked.

"I wanted to talk to Nate."

He lay the tray on the floor and handed a drink to each of us. My generous lesbian grabbed the empty tray and was about to leave, but Fox gestured for her to stay. From the living room, a muffled dance beat seeped through, and its distraction eased my erratic state of mind.

"You want to know about Ben?" I asked Fox.

"Yes. Do you think he loves me?"

"Oh yes!" Bev replied. "Any blind man can see that. I just hope you didn't use that dildo before you got here."

He chuckled like a toddler. "We almost did. Ben wanted to stay home and send it upward for its maiden voyage, but I wanted to party with his friends."

"Smart man. You want to show him that you fit in."

He verified her comment with a wink. "What makes you sure Ben loves me?"

"You heard what he said out there. He wants validation, and even though he aimed his comment at my nephew and Nate, it's you he needs validation from."

"She's right, Fox," I confirmed. "What are you waiting for?"

"That's rich coming from you, Nate." Bev's voice boomed.

"Okay, I was Mister Cautious when Cam and I started out, but he kept showing interest then acting single. Oh, I see your point. Ben's doing the same thing that Cameron did."

"Fox, I know gay men. They're still men with all that silly pride stuff, with a bit of girl thrown in. Ben might act alpha, just like you do, but you both want to be swept off your feet." She turned to me. "That's why you're going to Buenos Aires. Sweep my silly nephew off his feet." She turned back to Fox. "And you, soften your act and Ben will too."

Lucy raced in. "You have to see this," she said, grabbing my hand and pulling me off the floor.

Chapter Eleven

ROGER WAS NAKED. Almost. He had his apron on, but it still didn't hide the fact his ass sagged like elephant skin. What made it more obvious was that he was shaking his body to classic disco. Bits of him jutted out in all directions. The occasional nipple. A hairy thigh. Then he tried to vogue. His lack of coordination meant his hands slapped his own face, and his attempt at a sultry expression would've sent an altar boy screaming.

Ben was standing nearby, clapping in time as encouragement to Roger's original dance moves. Fox marched up to his potential boyfriend with his hand out. Ben took it, then swiftly placed his cocktail on the dining table. While the butler boogied like a madman, my friend took the redhead in his arms and swayed. Fox pressed his cheek to Ben's, and I watched with envy.

Cameron was observing me, still seated in front of Roger's laptop. He then looked at the screen and moved the mouse, probably adding a new song to the playlist. His attention returned to me. Lucy touched me on the arm and whispered.

"If Ben and Fox can find common ground, so can you and Cam."

"The problem is, I'm still in the dark about what's going on," I replied quietly. "He won't tell me."

"Just go over to him. It's a start."

When I reached him, I heard more erratic feet on the floor behind me. Lucy and Aunt Beverley must have joined the rest, but I didn't want to break my gaze with my boyfriend's.

"Can I dance with you?" I asked.

"Nathan, you can always dance with me, my dreamy Australian."

He stood, and as he wiggled his tush, I took his hand, pulled his glasses from his face, and moved his body against mine. I heard him take a staccato breath.

"What's the matter?" I whispered.

"Nothing. This is a perfect moment."

We rocked back and forth; my hand around his waist, his on my upper back. Lucy, Aunt Beverley, and Rog twisted their feet on the floor. My favorite lesbian began to vogue with more panache than the free-flowing butler. Lucy kept her rhythm, still with her drink in her hand. Fox and Ben swayed like an old couple, and here was I with a head start on the new lovers, trying to feel the love.

"What is it you can't tell me?" I murmured.

"Nate, not now. I promise I'll tell you shortly, but for the moment, I need this. I need to be in your arms."

"Cameron, why?"

"Because I need to feel like number one."

"You are number one."

I stopped, but my boyfriend urged me to continue moving. His eyes were teary, so he reached for his glasses on the table. I moved him away so they were out of reach and softly held the back of his head, pulling him securely against my cheek. There was dampness, but whatever this was about, I didn't want to spoil the moment. I was feeling his warmth, and it was nice to have that back.

"Cam, you know I love you."

"I know."

"And do you still love me?"

"I do, way too much."

"Then why am I in the doghouse?"

"I was really embarrassed when you couldn't stop talking about Elliot in front of my parents."

"Oh come on!"

"Sh."

"Oh come on, Cameron. My relationship with Elliot finished too soon, but someone had to be my new boyfriend. I couldn't be single forever."

Cheering and applause came from the disco dancers. Ben and Fox were kissing like lovers in a black-and-white movie, and for a moment, I thought Roger was getting an erection under his apron, but I forced myself not to look.

Lucy shared glances between Ben and me; a sense of hope that she could be the next to find love. I nodded, catching her thoughts. Then she gazed down her nose at me; my half-baked smile answering her concern over my *own* disconcerting romance.

Beverley looked our way, and although I didn't see Cam's expression, his aunt scrunched her forehead in reply. She gestured to him to take me away. A good time to talk in private.

But I wanted to stay and observe Ben and Fox as Cam tugged my arm. Love's arrow had pierced the heart of my long-time friend and his unsuspecting bonk buddy. The wounds caught them unaware, until neither could hide from themselves. That's how love should be. That's how it was with me and Elliot.

My boyfriend led me back to his room.

"I don't know the best way to say it so I'm just going to come out with it." Cam gazed at his feet. "You called me Elliot twice while we were in Barcelona, and once during our opening night party at the Art-Wear Shop. And you didn't even realize what you said." His eyes met mine again. "So when you went on and on about your ex in front of my parents, I felt I should cut my losses before you realized you didn't really love me."

"But I am in love with you."

"Yet you haven't fallen out of love with Elliot." His voice was wavering. The tears were being held back.

"Maybe I'm so comfortable with you—" I searched for what I was trying to say.

"You don't know how to finish that sentence. Was it 'I'm so comfortable with you that I mistake you for my ex'?"

"Cam, there are widows who eventually learn how to cook for one. I'm relearning how to be a couple again. Time will heal me."

"But I'm not your psychologist, Nate. And I'm not your rebound. I'm Cameron, your charming American, but now and again, I don't think that's enough."

"Stop crucifying me. I'm human, for goodness sake. I make mistakes. But loving you is not one of them."

"I suspect you *think* you love me, Nate!"

"Oh come on now! You're so used to thinking about yourself you don't give anyone else a chance."

"I've given you more than a chance. You moved in with me."

"And it's been great, hasn't it? We make love like amphetamine-injected rabbits."

"What?"

"We've painted New York red, time and time again. Roger loves me. Your aunt Beverley loves me. Everyone loves me. And in your circle, everyone loves me and you together."

"In *my* circle? Not *our* circle? See, you haven't fully committed."

"What the—! I moved to New York. That's commitment!"

Lucy raced in. "What's going on here?" she asked, catching her breath.

Cam and I glared at each other like the chiefs of two warring tribes.

"How are Ben and Fox?" I asked, still not breaking eye contact with my accuser.

"Your change of subject isn't going to work with me, Nate," Lucy said. "But you realize your dispute out there is what made Ben and Fox kiss in the first place? The tension had us all uncomfortable. Stop looking at each other like that! You look like you're going to murder each other."

The new lovebirds entered the room, holding hands.

"Is everything okay?" Fox asked.

"It doesn't look like it," said Ben.

"Everything's fine, guys." Cameron voice was monotone. "Forgive us. Nate and I just aren't on the same page."

He forced a smile for the others, then left the room without looking back at me. No one knew what to say, and as the room felt colder, I realized Cam was with his entourage in one room, and I was with mine on the other side of the battlefield.

Chapter Twelve

"DO YOU REMEMBER when I talked about my friend Phantom?" Fox asked.

"Your friend who died of a blood clot," Lucy replied.

"Yes, him." Fox gestured to the carpet. We all eased ourselves to the ground with Ben still holding Fox's hand. "I sat on the floor of my studio apartment for days, like we are now, rocking back and forth, hardly eating. At least when I was awake. I had sleeping pills on the coffee table next to me and medicated myself every time the pain was too harsh."

"You did what?" Ben barked.

"No, lover, I don't have suicidal tendencies."

"But still, you were taking a risk having them at hand," said Lucy.

"Yeah, I was foolish, but seriously, I was in control."

"I'm with them, Fox," I said. "You might have thought you were in control but—"

"What I'm trying to say is it fucking hurt. Dead friend. All of a sudden. Grief. Pain. The works!"

"Okay, sorry. So how are you coping with it?"

"Oh, I put that pain to bed."

The rest of us shared quick glances.

"How did you put that pain to bed?" Ben asked wearily.

"After three days on the floor and after running out of tablets—don't look at me like that, guys—anyway, I decided to have a ritual. So with a bottle of bourbon, a few of the things he gave me over the years, and some timber I stole from a building site, I borrowed a car and some camping gear and set out on my own personal mission.

"I traveled inland, looking for a spot and eventually found the quietest town I could. I drove into its backstreets, searching for somewhere. Just somewhere. And somewhere showed up. About half a kilometer was somewhere between nothingness and more nothingness. It was night by then so I set up camp." He laughed to himself. "I don't know if I told you this, but he used to call me Snake."

"You told us," Lucy replied.

"So I started a fire, warmed myself on bourbon, and stripped to my underwear. I placed the items he gave me over the years around the fire, but not too close, so nothing would burn. And then I started doing my own tribute in a snake dance, stepping around the books and old CDs he gave me and a picture of him in one of those rare moments he felt life wasn't a challenge. And I felt him there that night, thanks to the bourbon. And I sang his favorite awful pop tune."

Fox laughed some more, in between the tears.

"You're not over him yet, are you?" I kept my voice low as I asked.

"I am. I did what I did, and I got over it."

Ben moved to comfort Fox, but he waved him away.

"We had a ritual for Elliot," said Lucy. "At his gravesite. Just me, Ben, Nate, and a gay couple Elliot knew. Shit. We promised we'd catch up with Tony and Graham. We never have."

"I'm sure they understand," I said.

"Anyway, Nate gave this beautiful speech about the way different people make you feel, and how you want to share the way that person makes you feel with other people. So let me ask you, Fox, how did Phantom make you feel?"

"Needed."

"I need you." Ben began to stroke his boyfriend's flaming red hair.

"I need you too, Fox," I added. "Even if it's just to talk shit through."

"Well, hell!" said Lucy. "If they need you, I need you. I need you for Ben."

"I wish I had one of Roger's cocktails right now," I said.

"Go get one," Lucy suggested. "Oh, I get it, Nate. You don't want to face the enemy. I'll get you one."

"No, don't. We have to work tomorrow."

Lines of moisture made Fox's cheeks glisten. "I'm not really over Phantom."

"You said it, not us. But hey, I know how hard it is. Feelings aren't supposed to be logical. They're there to give us a reality check. I loved Elliot, and sometimes the past doesn't want to let go—"

"It has let you go, Nate," Ben interjected.

"I agree," said Lucy.

"It hasn't. Apparently, I've called Cameron Elliot several times by mistake."

"Ouch. Why do relationships have to be so complicated? Oops, sorry, Ben. Sorry, Fox. I'm sure yours will be the one we all envy."

"Regardless of how sickeningly in love you are, I just want to say, Fox, that dead people are always in your heart, and over time they get easier to deal with."

"You danced naked around a campfire for this guy," Ben teased. "Maybe we should shake our pink bits for Elliot."

Suddenly I couldn't stop smiling, but not from what Ben said.

"Thank you, Fox," I sung. Yes, seriously, I put a tune to it.

"For what?"

"This is going to sound inappropriate, but you've made me realize something about your ritual for Phantom."

"Well, out with it!" Lucy demanded.

"I'm more over Elliot than I thought. And definitely more over Elliot than Cam gives me credit for."

"I get it," said Fox. "You're more over Elliot than I'm over Phantom." He grinned just as Ben kissed his tearstained cheek.

"Hold on." Ben had the look of a good journalist not letting a politician off the hook. "You just said you called Cameron Elliot by mistake. In the scale of how *over* someone is, I think that rates pretty close to Fox and Phantom."

"No, I see Nate's point," Lucy reasoned. "Fox did his snake dance. All we did was go to the cemetery and toast Elliot with champagne. Nate didn't feel the need to tribal dance for Elliot, or write an aria or create a sculpture in his honor. I think in the 'letting go' scheme of things, Nate trumps Fox."

"I'm with Lucy," Fox replied. "Shit, look at me now, drying my tears. And hell, tears don't lie."

I winked at him. "Promise me something, Fox. Never ask me for tips on love. I want you and Ben to stay together."

He nodded.

"But as for me and Cameron, it's my journey—a journey I have to put back on track." I stood. "Come on."

The others followed me out of the bedroom.

Aunt Beverley and Roger were seated at the dining table. The butler was still naked under his apron and his dick was peeking out from under the material, but I tried not to look. I prayed the owners of the house steam-cleaned the soft furnishings every time their vacationing guests left.

Cameron was performing. There was no music, but still he did his own interpretation of a pop star waiting to be discovered, complete with a wooden spoon as a microphone, a drooling voice, and slow-motion moves.

Lucy, Ben, and Fox stared quizzically at me as if I was the pizza boy with a late delivery.

"He's stoned," I replied.

"The bong is over there," Aunt Beverley slurred. She pointed to the rainbow-colored glass implement near the exhaust fan in the kitchen.

"Pack your bags, darling," said Cam, his voice lighter than air.

"Why?" I asked.

"We're going to Buenos Aires!"

"When?"

"In two hours."

It was lucky that Cam and I wore the same size clothes, so there was no need to get back to Lucy's to pack. Lucy rushed to the bedroom and started cramming shirts and jeans into Cam's suitcase. I stuck my light-headed boyfriend under the shower and soaped him head to toe. In fifteen minutes, we were done. We ordered a cab so I could pick up my toothbrush and passport from Lucy's and then continue on. She, of course, would ride with us, simply to catch a lift home and sleep before work the next day.

We ran past Ben, who waved before taking a hit from the bong, and blew kisses to the others, not stopping for hugs.

Chapter Thirteen

CAMERON HAD SLEEPING pills in his pocket.

"Are you sure you should take those while you're still stoned?"

"They're for both of us, Nate. It's a long flight."

"Where did you get them?"

"Lucy gave them to me. She didn't want to give them to you because she knew you wouldn't take them."

I sat in my premium economy seat. It was the only class Beverley could get us at short notice. There were two hostesses looking after our small area, wrapped in designer black uniforms and handing out drinks like they were prizes.

"We should fly premium economy more often, Cam. This isn't bad. And it's cheaper."

"So, do you want to stay awake on this fifteen-hour flight and enjoy the service, or do you want to wake up for breakfast?"

"We should talk."

"Nate, I love you. You know that. Treat me like number one when we get to Argentina and I won't be a spoiled sook anymore. I promise."

We asked for sparkling water, received a puzzled look from the hostess, and quickly swallowed our tablets. Then I kissed him, and for a moment, some old magic was back. Either that or the sleeping pill was making me light-headed.

WE STEPPED OUT of our rented apartment building and onto the street. I looked up at its expanse. An ornate structure in widescreen. Railed balconies only large enough for one person to sneak out and have a cigarette, enclosed double-glass doors in symmetrical columns and rows over the six stories. Greek columns melded themselves into the structure, reminding us that Argentina was like Europe, without being in Europe.

I took its photo from the other side of the street.

"What are we doing today?" Cameron called, still in front of our building.

"We're off to find dulce de leche ice cream."

"What's that?"

"I'm not sure." I walked back to him. "I was talking to an old guy in the foyer while you shot back up to pee, and he told me to find this ice cream. Apparently, the Argentineans go nuts over it. He wrote down a few places to find it."

We took a few steps before Cameron stopped me.

"Nathan, regardless of everything else that's happened, I'm glad we're here."

I kissed him. There were a few onlookers on this street, but no gasps of horror. We continued to explore.

Soon we came upon a local market. A band played the music of gypsies in front of the stalls. A man stood clad in what was once his Sunday best, playing some kind of horn I'd never seen before. The rest were in their casuals, seated on cheap plastic stools, making the song swirl with an accordion and many guitars. Passersby couldn't help but stamp their feet, a little flamenco waking their souls if only for a moment.

The stalls were packed with a large number of leather goods. Bags, wallets, and purses filled every spare space. And color was a thing. No boring black for these customers.

"We're surrounded by dead cows," said Cameron.

"I also heard that every restaurant offers dead cow, and lots of it. Meat is the thing here."

"Who told you that?"

"That same guy that told me about dulce de leche ice cream."

I found a woman selling sensible secondhand clothes for all types of weather, and asked about the frozen delicacy. She pointed beyond the markets, telling us we weren't far from one of the best places. So we strolled.

"Ben and Fox have something special." I didn't expect Cam so say this.

"We do, or we did. I'd like to think we still do."

"They were all over each other like a rash."

"Just like we were the last time we were home in New York."

"Yeah, I guess you're right. You've made New York your home."

Flannelette caught my eye. A shop beyond the stalls had old-fashioned pajamas in its display window. They were from an era when men smoked pipes and wore robes with basic slippers.

"I *know* you're thinking what I'm thinking, Cam."

"Hey, we're gay men. Watching period drama is our birthright. Living it is our guilty pleasure."

We marched in like shoppers with a mission. We looked at every design, scrutinizing every pattern, or lack of it, and confirmed our choices with each other. Pale blue with white stripes. Basic navy. Green with a thin red line on the sleeves.

"This one!" Cameron shrieked. He held up a pair in coffee tones. They matched his eyes.

"Definitely!" I replied. "I can't decide between these two." One was dark blue while the other featured red and blue checks.

"Be bold. Take the checks."

I did. We walked out, proud of our purchases.

"You know, Cam, buying clothes just to hang around the apartment in is not something most people do. Most are happy with old T-shirts and track pants."

"Yeah, but it's cheap here. So why not? We're nesting, so now we have official 'hang about in' clothes."

His lover's smile came back. A grin I was glad had not been misplaced. I took it in for as long as I could, praying it would never fade.

"You light up when you smile," I said. "You always do."

"It's *your* smile that's infectious. I can't help it."

In a busy street of shoppers, we kissed. Eyes shut. Mouths moist. Love shared. *What on earth have we been arguing about?*

"There it is." Cam pointed past a busker with a harmonica. An ice-cream parlor was nearby. Excited children were bouncing outside, waiting to get their fix. We joined them in what was this country's mandatory addiction.

The toffee-colored delight crowned our cones. A treasure of milk and ice dripped down the wafer. Our kid-like pleasure of sticky fingers made us grin like maniacs. Then, the first lick. It was gooey and creamy and oh so caramel. Dulce de leche was Spanish for lush!

And so the day continued. We took in historical buildings painted pastel, ordered vegetarian meals covered in ham, and drooled over antique stores with wares from wealthy households. Before returning to our building, we binged on ice cream once more.

"There's something special about this city," said Cameron.

"Spoken like a true romantic."

"No, there's something here I haven't seen anywhere in America or Australia, or the places we've traveled."

"What?"

"Respect."

"Huh?"

I looked around. People old and young walked the streets. They talked and greeted each other as they did in any city. They gazed at shop windows and crossed the roads with caution. Whatever the class, whatever the age of the clothes they wore, they went about their business proudly. And that's when the penny dropped.

"The elders have the most pride," I declared. "They're looked up to. You can see it in the way they carry themselves."

"And they're not trying to look young. They wear the classics, and wear them well."

"No youth culture. We haven't been bombarded with pictures of what's cool. And all the clothes in the stores are from fashion's past."

"Nathan, I'm so glad I was stoned and drunk when Aunt Bev suggested this."

That smile, again. My charming American. My only love.

"Kiss me like you mean it, Cam."

"Upstairs."

We raced floor by floor, our shoes slapping the stone steps. As we panted heavily at our front door, we were greeted by the old guy who talked to me in the foyer earlier that day.

"It was Nathan, wasn't it?" His accent as charming as his nature.

"Yes, it is, and this is Cameron. I'm sorry, I forgot your name."

"Ruben," he replied. "Are you two in love?" His forehead scrunched while studying our faces. "Did I say something I shouldn't have? You're just friends?"

"No, you're right," said Cameron. "He's my boyfriend."

The way he said it should have made me smile, but it sounded more like a Wikipedia fact than a tender testimonial.

"Then you must come inside and meet Lucas." He placed his key in the lock of the apartment next door. "I'll make a cup of coffee, or maté, perhaps?"

Cam and I nodded.

"We'd love a coffee," Cameron said, knowing my preference.

And so we entered. Their place was as small as ours next door. It had a long room with a couch and kitchen in one area, and the TV and bed in the other. It was decked in dark carpet, which had decided to stop clutching onto the ground where it met the walls. There was an old smell too, as if generations of grandmothers also called this place home. Odors of Sunday roasts and winter stews hung about as if they were haunting this flat.

Lucas was reading a book. He placed it next to him on the sofa, the pages open facedown, and then stood. His wire-framed glasses gave him a sense of elegance, while his smile made me serene even with his butter-colored teeth. He extended his arm so we both shook his hand.

"Darling," said Ruben to his mate, "make us a cup of coffee."

Again, he smiled gently before making his way to the kitchen. Cameron and I sat on the sofa while Ruben faced us in an armchair. Beyond that, there was nowhere else to sit but on the bed.

"Where are you from?" our host asked.

"New York," I said.

"You don't sound like a New Yorker. You don't even sound American. British?"

"Australian."

"Did you meet in Australia or America?"

"Prague," Cam replied.

"Prague? You two sound like jet-setters. What brings you here?"

Cue awkward silence. Even Lucas stopped grinding the coffee beans, waiting for a reply.

"It's kind of a honeymoon," Cameron finally said.

"One of many," I replied, keeping my sarcasm in check.

"I sense trouble in paradise," said Lucas.

"Quiet!" Ruben commanded. "Young ones need encouragement."

"Encouragement? They've got it easy. In our day, we were hiding in the dark and kissing in the shadows. I don't know what they've got to worry about. They can hold hands in public!"

"Now, Lucas, you don't know what they're going through."

Not only had the coffee making come to a halt, now we were the center of their argument. And I really wanted a strong aromatic brew.

"Oh come on, darling, I can see what they're going through. They're being nice to an old man who's wishing he was young enough to bed them!"

"Not now, Lucas. Not now."

"I'd leave, boys, while you've still got your pants on."

"This is about that email, isn't it?"

Lucas addressed Cam and I. "Here I was with a sore elbow, and all he wanted to do was send an email. He turned on the computer and sent an email while I was in pain!"

"There is nothing wrong with your elbow, otherwise you wouldn't be making coffee."

"And your coffee is more important than my elbow."

Cameron stood. I followed his lead.

"No, sit, boys. This is one of our minor fights."

We stayed standing.

"I had to buy this coffee and the milk with my sore elbow. And what did you do? Send some majorly important email!"

"Please, Lucas, you're making our guests feel uncomfortable."

"Uncomfortable? I'm the one making the damn coffee!" He slammed the grinder on the bench, making half-ground beans jump and scatter. "Would you like a biscuit as well, boys? Shall I start baking with my sore elbow?"

"Don't mind our soap opera, boys," Ruben said coolly. His voice was as measured as a Shakespearian actor's. "Lucas loves drama."

"I must! I live with you."

"Now, boys, come back from the door. There's no need to leave." He turned back to his partner. "Is it because you don't feel in control? Is that what this is about? You want me to make the damn coffee so you can feel in charge?"

"That would be a great start. You always expect *me* to jump. You snap your fingers and order me around like I'm your pet."

"Come back, boys. See what you're doing? Did you find the dulce de leche ice cream?"

We shut the door behind us only to hear "Well, congratulations, you've won the Academy Award!" We dashed inside our apartment faster than a toupee blown by a hurricane.

"Let's never be like them," I said.

Cam answered with his lips. They brushed against mine, making me tingle, so I shut my eyes and kissed him. As I drank in my special man, something else decided to tingle. Another member of my physical form had something to say. Something to put right.

I felt his heat. An energy that was coming for me, wrapping me in need. I held him closer, yearning to be part of his being.

Addictions are hard to shake, even when there's distance between you and the thing you crave for. And you can fool yourself that there're a thousand reasons why it won't work, but bodies don't lie.

Cameron was rising. I pressed mine against his. And his groan was the start of where I wanted him. Of where we both needed to be.

Chapter Fourteen

YOU'VE GOT TO love tapas. Little plates of everything. Tender meatballs. Crisp haloumi. Garlic mushrooms with bite-size heads. Sensual tarts, cheesy and stringy. Seductive olives that roll in your mouth as you suck the flavor from them.

"You're doing that thing you always do when you look at food, Nate." Cameron slurred a little as he spoke.

"I'm tipsy," I noted.

"No, you're drunk."

"You're one to talk."

We were on the 'Out and About' pub crawl, a weekly event that brought gay and lesbian locals and tourists together. Thank god they were feeding us again. This was our third pub, and we were feeling the effects of our generous bartenders.

A guy in a ribbed white sweater and enough gel in his hair to fill a swimming pool, gave us the eye as he spoke to his fellow drunkard.

"I think my underwear just got its first coat," said Cameron.

"I like it when you're sleazy," I replied. "I like it better when you're sleazy at home, but I guess—"

"Come on, Nate. You also think he's hot."

I wanted to reply, but coherent thought and alcohol aren't best of friends. Of course I found him sexy. *But is this Cam's way of saying he is over me?* I thought about how passionate and connected we were the night before. *Am I fooling myself? Have we become friends with benefits?*

"Yeah, Cam, he's cute. But we'd slice our fingers running our hands through the sharp edges of his hair."

To my dismay, he wandered over with his mate. Both their gazes viewed us like we were the last Tim Tams in the packet.

"You got to admit, this is fun!" said the crispy-haired beauty.

"I'm Evan, and this is Jake," said his partner in crime.

"Nate and Cam," I replied. "It sounds like you're Canadian."

"That's right. And you're Australian?"

"Yes."

"But I'm from New York," Cam added.

"Oh, I thought you were a couple," said Evan.

"We are. He lives with me in Manhattan."

"We're among the jet set," said Jake.

I looked around for an out. A couple of middle-aged men with shaved heads stood by the bar, conversing passionately. A short florescent-haired lesbian was trying to see eye to eye with two towering gays. Another group of guys were showing each other pics on their phones. The bald ones were my best bet, but I couldn't leave Cam with these vultures.

"Are you together?" my boyfriend asked.

"Yes," Jake replied.

"How long have you been a couple?"

"Three years." They kissed briefly for show. "Three very satisfying years. You?"

"We're coming up to seven months," I replied.

"An Australian and an American. You left your beaches for skyscrapers."

"Pretty much."

"You look content," said Evan. But his face turned to doubt. Jake mirrored the expression.

"It's a good thing we're here," Jake declared. "See those two guys over there." He pointed to the middle-aged baldies. "Trust me, they know everything."

"They've caught it, tasted it, fucked it, and cried over it," said Evan. "Their words, not mine."

"Maybe we should talk to them for advice," I said. But a bearded local in an oversized coat had joined them.

"You're in luck, Nate," said Evan. "We have phonographic memories. Anything they know, we now know."

"Lesson number one," Jake began, "and this one we can personally vouch for. Beware the end of the honeymoon period."

"Say what?" This phrase jumped from my mouth like a hiccup.

"I think that's what's happened to Nathan," said Cam.

"What about you? You're as distant as Mars."

"Now, now, kids," Jake said. "This is good."

"How can this be good?" I asked.

"You're determined to talk it out. Lesson number two, always communicate."

I laughed for no reason. Oddly, so did Cam.

"Nathan, I think your *thing* about Elliot is something I've got to live with."

"Dangerous waters," Evan announced. "Should we leave you two to talk?"

"Elliot is my ex," I replied. "My dead ex. We never finished the relationship, but I've resigned myself that I never will. It's the past. This charming American here in front of me is my present."

"I'm either your friend or your lover," Cam replied. "Preferably both. And as a friend, I should help you through this. But you need to talk to me and not just Ben and Lucy all the time."

I swallowed hard.

"Your boyfriend has to be your friend too, otherwise he's just a lover." Jake looked me square in the eye as he said this.

"He's right," Cam said. "Remember what I was like when we met. I wasn't being your friend. I just thought boyfriends were automatic. You loved them. They loved you back. Then I fell deeper and knew I had it wrong."

"I was your friend from the start, Cameron. I always have been."

"Then trust me with your feelings about Elliot."

Cue screen kiss. I grabbed him by the lapels, pulled him to my lips, and held on to that moment, until—

"But you shunned me," I said, interrupting my own romantic gesture. "You asked me not to come home when I flew to Sydney."

"My shield went up. I already told you, Nate, I was cutting my losses."

"So why do you feel differently now?"

"Because I was seeing my world through fear. I know we have something beyond traveling to every corner of the earth imaginable. Roger and Aunt Beverley have been pounding sense into me every moment you've been away."

"I don't want to lose this, Cam, even if we didn't start our relationship on the right foot."

"Yesterday is yesterday, guys." Jake's cheeky demeanor was put on hold. "Evan and I can see you have something here. This is day one of the rest of your lives. Okay, I know that sounds clichéd, but work with me. You wouldn't be putting each other through this bump in the road if your relationship didn't matter."

I was beginning to like these Canadians.

"Where do we go from here?" Cam asked.

"Don't have sex while watching porn," Jake replied.

"What?"

"Seriously," Evan continued. "Make love in bed, that way you concentrate on each other. You don't want your relationship to play out in the fantasy world of your imaginary sex partners."

The couple's lips met, their moment to lose themselves from our woes.

"And kiss, guys," Jake said quietly. "Kiss often and regularly."

"And don't always be the first to come," Evan blurted. "Seriously, don't look at me like that. I know Jake's dirty talk."

"He does. Sometimes I'm turning myself on. Sometimes I'm turning Evan on. It's in what I say. And it doesn't matter if we both don't come, as long as we're sharing."

Cam and I both wore ridiculous grins. "No more porn," I repeated.

"Not even that one with the Swedish guy and the melon baller?" Cam asked.

"As long as you don't screw in front of the TV," Evan replied. "Watch the Swedish guy, then go to bed and play. Um, what's he do with the melon baller?"

"Did the bald couple tell you anything else?" Cam pointed to them as he said this, his finger waving in the air like a branch swaying in the breeze.

"Something about sitting around the house in pajamas," Jake replied. "They said feeling cozy saved their relationship."

"How?"

"They didn't explain."

"It's about contentment," I answered. I pictured Cam in the sleepwear we bought.

"But their main point was the honeymoon period thing. And the seven-year itch, which they promised to expand on at the next pub."

"Drink up, queers!" called our commander from the bar. His arms shot to the heavens like a stripper jumping out of a cake. "It's time for the next pub."

"This conversation has made me feel sober," I said.

"Don't kid yourself," Evan replied. "You'll either forget most of it, or remember it as if you were coherent. And trust me, none of us here are coherent."

"As long as I remember the bit about the honeymoon period."

"The honeymoon period!" one of the baldies exclaimed as he and his mate sauntered past. "Just remember—" He looked to Evan and Jake until they pointed to us. "Just remember, all couples fall out of the honeymoon period, but it's up to you to either fail or succeed—and if you don't grow together, you're both going to retreat into who you were when you were single."

His partner scrutinized us before saying, "So go past this point and see where it takes you!"

EVAN WAS STRUGGLING with his rendition of "Loving You" by Minnie somebody-or-other at the next venue—a karaoke bar. At a point where he took a breath and our ears stopped begging for mercy, someone let loose with a ripper fart.

Without missing a beat, he turned toward the sound and cried, "Everyone's a critic!"

Applause and laughter followed, while Jake blew a kiss.

"Now that's love," said Titan, one of the baldies who had strolled with us to this club.

Since entering the next phase of drunkenness, Titan and his partner, Piers, were advising Cam and I further in the art of a successful relationship. Jake and Evan had kept quiet for this part of the conversation, picking up new tips from the masters. With the final verdict on Evan's lack of singing talents declared so openly, he joined us for more counseling.

"Twenty-three years is a long time," I said. "How do you not kill each other?"

"By doing what you and Cameron seem to be doing—fighting," Piers answered. "Arguments are important, as long as they don't get personal. Keep telling each other how you feel. Never stop. Also, make sure you kiss and make up by the time you go to sleep." He placed his hand on my boyfriend's shoulder. "And Cameron, if you need time out, don't do it when the person you love is halfway around the world."

Cam nodded sheepishly.

Another potential star clutched his beer while he meandered toward the stage. Splashes of liquid amber wet the floor. "Stay away from the spotlight," called one of his colorful tribe. "Trust me, the light is not your friend." With a grin and an upturned finger, he continued to the microphone.

Unintelligible lyrics boomed from the speaker until, abruptly, he crashed to the ground. More unintelligible lyrics were sung from the deck without amplification. Then real music filled the room as the last of the karaoke warriors was dragged from the stage by his posse.

"Can I ask you guys a question?" I asked.

"You've been asking questions since we got here," said Titan.

"How do you keep it fresh after the honeymoon period?"

Cam sidled up to me.

"You keep dating," Piers replied. "And you keep dating all through the relationship."

"The trick is to invest in one another so much, there's no reason to try and rekindle the feeling of those early years by having an affair," Titan added. "Because you are having an affair, with your boyfriend!"

"Do it right and that honeymoon period keeps getting rediscovered as you grow older."

They chuckled, sounding like they were both embarrassed.

"I know a nervous laugh when I hear one," Jake alleged. "What aren't you telling us?"

"It's nothing," Titan replied.

"Come on. What is it?"

"Yeah, come on, guys," said Cameron. "We need to hear from our gay elders."

"Okay," Piers replied as he lifted his wineglass like he was accepting an award. "We had the same conversation last night with a miserable old couple who live here."

"They argued like politicians," Titan added.

"And even after our spiel about the continuous honeymoon period, they went on and on about the things that annoy each other."

"Then we talked about the things we get annoyed about. Like the fact that Piers never puts dirty dishes in the dishwasher." Our bald advisor said this with joy.

"Or having to hold Titan's head as he throws up in the toilet." A loving grin followed his words.

"Or the way Piers never empties used hankies from his jeans when he throws them in the laundry basket."

"Or having to hold Titan's head as he throws up in the street."

"Or how Piers leaves the shoes he's worn all over the house."

"Or waking up to hold Titan's head while he throws up in the bucket next to the bed."

"And these are the things that if for whatever reason, your husband is not around, you will miss the most."

"And sometimes leaving shoes around the house or hankies in pockets is your way of showing you care."

I looked at Cameron. "Like leaving the toothpaste and the deodorant on the sink after you've used them."

"Or never taking out the garbage," he countered.

"Or waking me up for sex in the middle of the night," said Jake.

"I'm not the only one guilty of that," Evan replied.

"I think our work here is done," said Titan to his partner. "Our students get an A plus."

"Another round of drinks, boys?" Piers asked, and wandered to the bar before we could reply.

The mishmash of queer locals and tourists had done the rounds, each conversing with everyone at least once throughout the night. And there was still one more nightclub to go. Jake told us that at this last bar you could order a cocktail with 80 percent vodka and 20 percent orange juice, if you had the money. And all of us here exchanging first-world currency had the money.

I watched the fluorescent-haired lesbian as her fingers moved gently against the cheek of a local girl she'd met at the last pub, while the tall gay guys were already locking lips like hungry men. Piers smiled as he observed them, with the grin of someone who'd just discovered love.

Titan waved us in like a footballer signaling his teammates to huddle closer. "And if you take all of our advice, kissing will always feel passionate, even a peck on the cheek, and your boyfriend's lips will always be your addiction."

Chapter Fifteen

THERE ARE ALL kinds of sex. Sex that makes you want to sing from the balcony and tell the world what you just did. Sex that makes you feel dirty in a good way. Sex that makes you feel so ravenous you want to devour your partner. Sex that just feels wholesome and natural no matter where you stick what.

Then there is sex that leaves you unsure.

A trail of discarded clothes paved a path to our bed. We were more than drunk. We were animals of hair and flesh, while our minds were focused on any body part that had a job to do. I was licking whatever came my way, then losing myself in the cavern of his mouth. Tongues on the attack. Grunting like tribesmen playing out a ritual.

I kissed his skin from thigh to groin. A little wet patch was waiting—a little juice to tempt me. So I pressed my lips against what was pink and luscious.

And all through this, I felt disconnected. *Is this Cameron?* This could have been anyone. Just two plastered gay men doing what they do best.

HE SLEPT. I sat on the couch by myself, peering at the night sky. My head was in that lucky period—the time before the mother of all headaches would rip my sozzled skull from my shoulders and smash it like a pumpkin against the wall.

The words of Titan, Piers, Jake, and Evan swam in circles behind my red eyes. Things you hate. Things you love. Not watching porn. Or was it not watching porn before sex? Praise the melon baller!

I stood. Carefully, I made my way to Cameron. He held his pillow like a toddler holds a teddy bear, close to his heart. I closed my eyes because watching him made me feel like crying.

"I like to think of you as my charming American," I whispered. "But in the recent past, I haven't been sure you're my charming anything." He stirred so I walked away, sat back on the couch, and spoke to no one. "When I first met you, Cam, I was envious of your lifestyle. Mostly because you didn't work for it. But then I got to know your vulnerabilities, which made me love even more, once I figured out how to handle them.

"And yes, you're right. I have to talk to you about the way I feel about Elliot. I have to talk. I have to talk. I have to—"

My words started to have a drowsy tone.

"We've spoken in Sydney and here in Buenos Aires, but I'm still not sure where we, or I for that matter, stand. Have the baldies and Jake and Evan got their relationship right? And are we just kidding ourselves that we are in love? Shit, even Ben and Fox look more like a couple than us."

I shut my mouth. I imagined life without Cameron. I felt a kick to the stomach.

"Yeah, I'm in love with you, my charming New Yorker, but I'm scared it may not be enough."

Chapter Sixteen

WE WERE WARNED to only hail one taxi company, and a couple of days after nursing killer hangovers, we ventured into the night, making sure we got into the right cab.

"Why do we have to stick with this company?" I asked.

"I'm not sure, but Aunt Bev insisted on it."

"Where?" asked our driver.

"Tango Entre Muchachos, San Telmo."

"Ah. Gay?"

"¡Si, señor!"

And off we went like a rocket ship dodging enemy laser fire. I held on to the door as we swerved through backstreets while lights streaked past as if they were comets. Faces made fast impressions as the cast of Buenos Aires were unaltered by the antics of another reckless cab driver.

"Slow down," Cam commanded. But the words were forced back down his throat.

My insides felt like they were being whisked in an electric mixer, ready to be baked at three hundred degrees Fahrenheit. Our seat belts were keeping us from flying through the windscreen. Finally our driver pulled up to our destination. I literally sighed.

"It's a gay hotel," I said.

"Yes, this is where it's held."

Cam paid as I hurried out of the car. I readjusted my hair in front of a window, trying to stay sexy for our date.

"That's what I love about you, Nate. You never calm down completely. You look good, trust me."

He stood in a burgundy shirt, ultra-tight jeans, and an approving look. A look that had become synonymous with this trip. A glance that said I was still valued but things were not the same. The wind had changed direction. Its sense of awe had gone. For an uneasy second, I wanted Cam and Nate to be new again.

I reached for his hand and tried to kill the image in my head—the words *The End* writing themselves in a wavy font in front of a lowered gray curtain.

"You're the New Yorkers," screamed a short guy, camp enough to wear a pink wedding dress and carry it off. "Did you survive the taxi ride?"

"Just," I replied.

He waved us inside the building. "You caught the right cab. Any other company and you might have been mugged."

Inside, gents of all shapes and sizes were practicing their steps. Arms around waists. Arms around shoulders. Mustaches, chic beards, and a lot of confused feet.

I undid the top button on Cam's shirt and gave him more than just an approving look. He smiled back as I quickly kissed his forehead.

"I'm your instructor, and as you can see, you have some catching up to do. Now, who's bitch and who's butch out of the two of you?"

"I'll be bitch this time," I said.

"That's what I like to see. A man who knows his place." He clapped his hands thrice. "Okay, come together, guys. We have some dancing to do."

FOR HALF AN hour, I kept knocking my knee against Cam's while moving my foot forward when it should have been going to the side.

"You're not here, are you, Nate?"

"Of course I'm here. We're on a date."

"No, Nate. Be honest. What's on your mind?"

I moved my arm from his waist and held his hands.

"Are we over, Cameron?"

"Over?"

"You asked me to be honest. So be honest with me. Is this the final chapter of Nathan and Cameron?"

His silence scared me. Around us, gypsy music from a trio of joyful men kept this room of gays laughing and dancing in synchronization. Yet *our* tango had ceased.

"We should keep moving, or we'll draw attention to ourselves." My words were said in silent terror.

"I don't think we feel like dancing."

"I don't think you feel like talking either."

"I've talked, Nathan. I've talked."

"Yes, you have. Mostly about me and Elliot."

"Let's sit."

We walked past the instructor who called, "Hey, where are you—" When he stopped, his comic look of concern disappeared. His efforts to make us laugh were lost.

We sat on a bench in the corner as all the merriment disappeared from our senses.

"I have a confession to make, Nathan."

"Don't break my heart. I'd rather not hear it."

"You're overanalyzing, Nate. I confess I built a wall around myself. I hid behind it when you left for Sydney, and I've had trouble breaking it down completely since we've been in Buenos Aires."

"We've had great sex while we've been here. There should be no wall."

My boyfriend stared past me; his code for requesting silence.

"Okay, sorry, Cam. I'm listening."

"The wall is to protect myself just in case I finally have to face…"

"Face what?"

"This is hard. I might have to face that I don't measure up to your last relationship."

I held him close. His head pressed against my chest while I chose my words, as this conversation would mean life or death.

"I'm at fault here, Cam. I don't want you to ever feel like second best, and you're right about what you said the other day. I talk about Elliot to Ben and Lucy. But if I talk about Elliot with you, I'm scared I'll drive you away."

"How can I be your boyfriend if you can't see me as a friend?"

"I do, Cameron. I do."

"I don't measure up."

I placed my finger under his chin and pulled his face up so I could see it. There were tears, not unlike mine. Several drops escaping the pain.

"You measure up, Mr. Cameron Charlton, you fucking measure up!"

"You don't see it, Nate. You're the one with all the power."

"I live at your place, in New York. I'm the kept man."

"But you could walk away at any moment and still land on your feet. You're a survivor. I'm not. I live on Daddy's handouts."

"We both live on Daddy's handouts, and he doesn't like it much."

It was great to hear Cam laugh. "I have to make the Art-Wear Shop a success. I need to show him I'm a success."

"It's our problem. We both have to make it a success."

"But I have to show you I can do it as well, Nate."

"No, it sounds like you need to show yourself you can do it."

"I don't believe I can." His voice squealed on the last word.

My boyfriend's face was that of a man trapped in the basement. Somewhere a boogieman was lurking, a father figure who never encouraged Cameron to fly.

"Was your dad always a grumpy old man?"

"No, money changed him."

"That's why I love you, Cam. Money is second nature to you. Let me help you be your own person."

"If you let me help you see that I'm worthy of your love, just like Elliot was."

"You are more than worthy! Coming here tonight, I thought this would be our last date. I would fly back to Sydney, or we'd just spend a few days doing our own thing or..."

"Or we'd drift apart."

"Better here than back in New York."

"You're not getting rid of me that easily, Nathan Jones."

The sound of the tango drifted into my senses as we kissed. Romance was around us and within us. The dance of passion and the truth in our souls were a potent combination.

"I'm glad we're talking," I confessed.

"Yeah, not talking hurts too much. Actually, seeing as we're being honest, I need to tell you Evan and Jake wanted a foursome the other night."

"What?"

"They asked me in one of the pubs—which one I can't remember. I said no."

"I'm glad you did. It might have put the nail in our coffin."

"I'm glad we got advice from Titan and Piers. They had a lot to share."

"Cameron, you know I'm not as confident in myself as I should be. Can we do everything they said?"

"Nathan, I was selfish for not talking about my fears and putting you through hell. I'm sorry."

"I was selfish for the whole Elliot thing."

"It's official. We're a tragic couple. All kissy kissy and huggy huggy."

"It's better this way, otherwise I really believe we would have drifted apart." I moved my head from his chest. "I'm serious. We would have sorted out our own feelings and licked our own wounds. And we'd both simply be each other's past boyfriend."

"What scares me about that is you're right. Our honeymoon period is over. This is for real now." Cam seemed spooked. "Promise me we'll always talk."

"Promise me we'll never have sex while watching porn."

We grinned.

"Promise me we'll sit around the apartment in our pajamas."

"Promise me we'll never stop dating."

"Promise me we'll always talk, or argue."

Around us, twenty or so couples had mastered the art of the tango while we rediscovered each other on the sideline.

"Come on, boys," called the instructor across the room. "You've kissed and made up, now dance!"

Cameron stood and reached for my hand, auburn eyes making me feel this was our first meeting. We took to the floor, my hand on his shoulder, his arm around my waist. And we synced, sliding along like champion skaters, zigzagging among the other couples.

His glasses gave him that air of Argentinean maturity. A local trait that favors the distinguished man. His assertive dance moves gave him flair and grace, the kind that only comes from leaving the boy behind. We were both men and proud of it, in each other's arms, telling the world we were in love.

"Perhaps a relationship is about two imperfect people who never want to give up on each other," Cam whispered.

"I think you're right. That's the secret. So through our actions, let's help each other grow. Let's bring out what's perfect in each other, then never look back."

I glanced at the others sharing their newfound tango steps and saw a ghost with a blond curl. He danced with a man in a checked shirt. My Elliot didn't see me or look around at the other guys in the room. He was hypnotized by the charm of this man whose bushy mustache could have swept a kitchen floor. But Elliot wasn't fazed. He kissed that man as if no one was watching.

"Bringing out the best in each other and never looking back." I repeated myself, and as I did I gazed at Elliot one last time. "I know how to bring out the best in another person. I've done it before." Once I finished the sentence, Elliot faded away.

Seeing him this time didn't leave a lasting impression. I was happy for my ex, and that was that. He belonged to a different time, my past. And eventually, the past is where you no longer live.

"I need to say something else, Nate," said the boyfriend in my arms. "We need to come up with a better name for the Art-Wear Shop."

I met his eyes. "You know, I've been thinking the same thing for a long time."

"How did we come up with that name?"

"I can't remember. I honestly can't."

"It's official. We're changing that awful name." He began to boogie. With everyone in full tango mode, my Cameron was busting a move to a gypsy tune.

And he was doing this for me. I might have had my last tango with Elliot a long time ago, but the man in front of me had a crazy dance of love. And whether he waltzed with the millionaires of New York, tangoed with pride in Buenos Aries, or boogied the discos of Sydney, I'd be there by his side, learning all the right moves.

About the Author

Kevin lives with his long-term partner, Warren, in their humble apartment (affectionately named Sabrina), in Australia's own "Emerald City," Sydney.

From an early age, Kevin had a passion for writing, jotting down stories and plays until it came time to confront puberty. After dealing with pimple creams and facial hair, Kevin didn't pick up a pen again until he was in his thirties.

His first novel spawned a secondary character named Guy, an insecure gay angel. Many readers argue that he is the star of the Actors and Angels book series. Guy's popularity surprised the author.

So with his fictional guardian angel guiding him, Kevin hopes to bring more whimsical tales of love, life, and friendship to his readers.

Facebook: https://www.facebook.com/DramaQueensWithLoveScenes

Twitter: https://twitter.com/kevinklehr

Website: https://kevinklehr.com

Also by Kevin Klehr

From Top to Bottom

Actors and Angels Series

Drama Queens with Love Scenes
Drama Queens and Adult Themes
Drama Queens and Devilish Schemes

Also Available from NineStar Press

www.ninestarpress.com